The Legend of League Park

Amy Stilgenbauer

Cover Image: Postcard of League Park in Cleveland, OH; Circa
1911; Braun Post Card Co. [Postcards of Cleveland, Cleveland
Memory Project, Cleveland State University Library;
www.clevelandmemory.org]
Used with permission of the Cleveland State University Library

ACKNOWLEDGMENTS

The Ragersville Historical Society; The Tuscarawas County
Historical Society; The Lakeview Cemetery Staff; University of
Michigan; Cleveland State University; Ball State University;
The Association of Women in Sports Media; and a variety of
historians, baseball players, fans, and writers who were willing
to share their experiences with me.

DEDICATION

For the girl who cried when they tore down Tigers Stadium and her little girl, who should always believe she can be anything she wants to be.

"If you tell a girl she can't play baseball, what else will she believe she can't do? This is the greatest game on earth, so why shouldn't we all play it?"

-Justine Siegal, the first woman to throw Major League batting practice

PROLOGUE: JACKIE

There is one story that above all others holds dear fascination for female baseball aficionados. They tell it to their friends, their daughters, their families, those guys at the bar who refuse to compute that a woman could comprehend athletics, everyone that they know. It is a story they tell with pride no matter how disappointing the ending. It is the story of Jackie Mitchell.

Virne Beatrice "Jackie" Mitchell Gilbert was a minor league pitcher on a double A team in Tennessee, the Chattanooga Lookouts, in 1931, when the Lookouts were scheduled to play an exhibition game against the New York Yankees. She was good. She was very good. There was no denying it, and it was hard not to be good when you were taught by Dizzy Vance. Still, how she must have felt being a seventeen year old facing down men who would be written in the history of baseball as some of the absolute greatest, the women who eagerly tell her story can only speculate.

What kind of nerves must she have felt being brought in as a reliever to face Babe Ruth? By that time, everyone in America already knew his name and what he was capable of. There was no way she could have known that a few pitches later, everyone would know hers. What kind of elation must she have felt hearing the crowd roar after striking out the famous slugger in only four pitches? And Lou Gehrig in only three? What seventeen year old rising sports star could feel anything but a sense of accomplishment at that? In that instant, she must have known she was going places.

Babe Ruth must have sounded little more than sour grapes to her when he threw down his bat and called the umpire a few choice names. In that moment, none of it could have mattered. She had performed a great baseball feat; one that was rarely replicated by other pitchers, no matter their gender.

Unfortunately those who regal their listeners with this moment from Jackie's life also have to deal with the bitterly worded aftermath, in which the commissioner voided her contract and declared women unfit to play baseball. It was "too strenuous" he is said to have claimed.

The ban lasted until 1992.

But it wasn't Jackie's fault. She was an extraordinary woman ahead of her time and her story has inspired so many who have come after to say, "Women can do it too. Just like Jackie Mitchell did."

PART ONE: GIOIA

1

Gioia's dresser and the wall behind it resembled something more like a shrine and it was one her friends didn't quite understand. Most of them couldn't tell you anything about the men in the framed card-stock pictures nor could they recognize the majority of the stadium photographs. Over time they had learned not to ask about the set up, because Gioia, however, could rattle off the statistics of each player and location of each ballpark by heart. It was her one true passion. Not even her baseball playing brother, Marco, quite understood.

"You know, I really don't think Petco Park deserves a spot on your wall of honor," he said plucking the photograph off the wall.

Gioia rolled her eyes. "You don't think you'd be happy to be there?" she asked. "I'd be happy to play anywhere."

He scoffed. "What would you know? You've never been out of Ohio."

She hopped down from her bed and walked over to the wall. "That's what all this is about," she said with a grand gesture at the pictures. It wasn't so much the look of the ballparks. It was what they represented. They were the homes of baseball, where the game that meant so much to her was played. There was something special about that.

"I still don't...get it." He frowned. Reasoning with his sister, especially on baseball related matters was a fruitless task. "I thought the wall was for places like Fenway."

"It's for all of them." She took the picture of the baseball stadium out of her brother's hand and repositioned it in its rightful place.

Marco scoffed again, leaning back against a relatively empty area of the wall. He stretched himself a little trying to take up as much space as his lean form would allow and raked a hand through his dark brown hair. "You have practice tonight?" He asked, partly in an effort to change the subject.

"Nah." She said immediately, but then thought a minute before adding, "I figured I'd go down to the field anyway though. Get in shape for fall ball without too many people around."

"Gonna overwork yourself." He laughed, but the concern did seem sincere. "If there's one thing I've learned..."

"Yes, Mr. Double A, please enlighten me."

Marco leveled a glare at his sister, but he knew the teasing was only meant playfully. "I was just thinking..."

"Gonna overwork yourself," she parroted gleefully.

He ignored her teasing. "Your classes are starting up again next week?"

Gioia sighed and nodded. "Please don't remind me." She wasn't exactly looking forward to her senior year. It came with far too much additional baggage.

"Then, since it's probably our last shot this season....what do you say you and I go up to the city tonight and take in a real game?" He wiggled his eyebrows knowingly. He knew that if there was one thing his little sister would never refuse, it would be the prospect of a major league game.

Try as she might, Gioia was not able to hide the way her eyes lit up at the idea. "I suppose we could." Her voice had a forced nonchalance, but Marco could see right through it. He knew exactly how much she wanted to be at every game and exactly how much she hated the fact that Bolivar was just far enough away from Cleveland to not make a habit out of it. She had regaled him on this many times. He was pretty sure she had even charted the exact mileage.

"Come on," he pretended to plead. "It's been too long since I just got to watch a game."

Gioia laughed. "I thought all you did was watch."

"Shut up. You know what I mean."

"All right," Gioia said with a smile, pointing at the picture in the center of the wall the one that had its location embellished with die-cut stars: Cleveland's Progressive Field. "The city tonight," she said, letting her glee show through. "Maybe we can even get Padre to go."

As if on cue, there came the sound of a door opening and slamming shut, followed by a deep voice calling from downstairs "Marco! Gioia!"

Gioia pushed past her brother, shoving him perhaps a little harder than she meant to out of the way, and rushed almost childishly down the stairs. "Padre..." she began.

He laughed at the excitement on her face. He couldn't help it. She looked like she used to on Christmas morning when she was five years old. It took a lot to get that look out of her now that she was a teenager. "What's all this about?"

"Marco says he's going to take us to a game tonight."

"Us?"

"If...you're off work tonight, that is," Gioia backtracked quickly. Mr. Rinaldi worked two jobs: tech support by day and grounds- keeping by night, it made making time for things like spontaneous road trips to Cleveland difficult.

He paused, considering. "I just drove by the fields and they are a swamp again. Too much rain."

Gioia wondered if that meant grounds work was deemed necessary or unnecessary. "Good thing I didn't try to go down there tonight," she said, opting for a more neutral answer.

"You're going to wreck your arm," Mr. Rinaldi said, in almost the same voice her brother had, as he shook his head and started for the kitchen.

She wanted to protest about how hard she needed to work, how she needed to be better than not only the other girls, but also all of the boys. A girl in sports couldn't just be good, she had to be the best, the absolute best. However, all she could manage to say was "Don't eat anything. We'll get food at the game. Please?"

"I didn't say I was able to go," he replied, but he put back the container of cheese which he had just removed from the refrigerator with a sigh. "We'll have to hurry if we want to make it to Cleveland by the first pitch."

2

The train was crowded on the way in. Gioia had to smile at all the red and blue caps that surrounded them as the Rapid made it's way underground to the Tower City station. She loved the rush, the excitement, every ounce of their ritual. From the drive to the station and then all the way in as the crowd made its way like a massive snake of people up through the mall, across the walkway with its view of the Cuyahoga train yards. With every step toward the field, there was a sense of exhilaration. Soon they would be in the sacred space where the baseball she'd loved since birth was played.

She could remember her first game in the stadium, when it was still shiny and new. Now, she was no longer clinging to her father and mother by the hand, and there were different faces on the banners that decorated the stands, but not much had changed otherwise. Not in her mind.

It was all quite the sight to behold: the road running by the river, the flags, the statues, the superstitious cemetery across the street. Even the fact that Yankees fans seemed to be streaming in as well, didn't interfere with the transformative nature of the experience.

"Time to offer up something to Joastat?" Marco suggested, noting those same Yankees fans with a touch more pessimism than his sister.

Gioia rolled her eyes. "I'm not -that- superstitious."

"Oh, but if we don't nod to your precious statue..."

"Gentleman and lady," Mr. Rinaldi interrupted, appearing with three freshly purchased tickets. "We're going to have to get inside."

He cast a look up to the logo adorning the field in an almost nostalgic way. Gioia and Marco smirked at each other as Marco mouthed, "Three, two, o-"

"It'll always be The Jake to me." The two Rinaldi siblings both nodded. He always said that.

Marco took his ticket and examined it carefully. "Behind home plate?" He teased.

Gioia knew better than to say such a thing, even as a joke. She knew very well that was a dearly held dream of her father's, but that right now it wasn't likely. Such seats were out of their price range. "Thank you, Padre."

"Maybe next time," He said with a light laugh. "When Marco is providing the tickets."

Marco blushed a little. "I'm not so sure about that, Padre." There was an awkward silence as they walked in and up to the bleachers. The two Rinaldi men had very different opinions of Marco's future prospects. They tried not to talk about it too often.

It was hard to fight the urge, however, with Mr. Sneering Yankees fan seated in front of the family. Mr. Rinaldi had made the mistake of commenting on how he had never been able to attend an away game, only to be informed that the Yankees fan was a born and raised Clevelander who'd never been to New York. Gioia tried not to remark on the betrayal, but a pronounced scoff may have given her away. After that, every time the Yankees scored or caught a fly ball or pitched a strike or anything at all in their favor, he would look back with a grin that had "I told you so" written all over it. It was almost as though with each New York play, he was insinuating that he had chosen the better team. It was debatably true that season, but it felt a little mean spirited all the same.

Gioia wanted to bitterly inform him that her brother was a top prospect for Cleveland and that he was going to turn the team around. When she opened her mouth to do so, however, Marco intercepted and leveled a venomous glare at her. "You're too modest," she muttered.

"Don't poke the tiger, he could break your neck," Marco replied with little more than a shrug.

"He's not a Tiger. He's a Yankee."

Marco didn't laugh, but their father did. Gioia could have sworn she heard the man in front of them chuckle too.

He looked back again when Cleveland allowed an uncaught fly ball to get into the corner, leading to a unnecessary triple. The half grin, half sneer was dripping with smugness "So?"

"Left fielder's a bum," Mr. Rinaldi said with a shrug.

Gioia interjected, "You say that about everyone, every time too. Even the people you like."

"Well, this time, I mean it."

"You also always say that!"

Marco laughed at the exchange between his father and sister. "You two, a man would think you guys manage the
team."

"Maybe we should," Gioia said proudly.

"We haven't even gotten started," their father said at the same time.

To their surprise the Yankees fan in front of them smiled the first genuine smile he had all night. "You remind me of my daughter when she was younger."

"Was she a Yankees fan too?" Gioia asked, arms crossed in a slightly defiant way.

He laughed lightly. "No. She liked Cleveland, just like her grandfather...and the Red Sox, just to annoy me, being a typical teenager."

Mr. Rinaldi smiled as well. "Gotta be a rebel somehow, right?" He nudged Gioia a bit at that. "This one here..."

"Padre!" Gioia whined. "Pick on Marco, please..."

The Yankees fan just smiled. "You're lucky. I miss her very much." He didn't say more to them, but a strange camaraderie suddenly invaded. His smirk for the rest of the game was quite different, less smug somehow.

Cleveland lost 10-6, but the crowd still seemed exuberant as they made their way back to the train, even the arguments and angry rants against the players, managers, owners, and peanut vendors had a sense of joy to them. The spell of the ballpark had not yet dissipated. Sometimes it was enough for them to be at the game and get their mind off the world for awhile, to not have to think about the pile of troubles waiting at home. That was certainly how it worked for the Rinaldis.

It was late before they arrived back in Bolivar, still talking about the game. This was par for the course. Gioia would never stop talking about it unless someone somehow actively silenced her. "Did you see his form when he slid into that catch? It was practically perfect."

Mr. Rinaldi smirked indulgently at his daughter. "Yes, you did mention that."

"I couldn't believe it." She could have kept going on for quite a bit longer.

"Enough shop talk for tonight, Gioia," Marco insisted as he started off up the stairs to his room. "I'm tired."

"Your form could use a little work, Marco," She teasingly called after him.

Their father interrupted quickly, hoping to put an end to it all for the night. "Both of you! Save it for the boys in Akron."

Marco shook his head and disappeared from sight. "Of course, Padre."

Gioia didn't say anything as she slipped up to her room as well, but she appreciated that he left her in the same category as Marco. The thought that her baseball knowledge would be of any use in Akron was heartening to hear. That was almost exactly where she wanted to be.

When she got to her room and closed the door behind her, she looked over at the wall of photographs. "Someday," she said to herself, pacing over and plucking a few off the wall at random, moving them around. It was a ritual; perhaps it seemed odd, but it comforted her to change their formations from time to time. Maybe if certain ballparks were in different positions, her teams would do better. Or, the thought did cross her mind from time to time that maybe her chances would be better too.

Her dear friend, Nellie Dessecker, always mocked the fact that baseball was such a superstitious sport. "You never hear football players talking about stadium ghosts," she would say. But it didn't matter to Gioia. It made her feel like she had an ounce of control over something in her life. It had been hard to get that feeling from anything else, especially with the impending end of her high school career coming up. That meant college, which she couldn't even imagine going to, let alone affording, was also coming up. That also likely meant the end of her chances to play ball herself. An athlete had to be really good to keep going. Marco had been lucky. He managed to get a couple academic scholarships to Akron University and a lot of playing time with the Aeroes while he was there. He couldn't play for the Zips like he had originally wanted (NCAA rules prohibited that), but in scheme of things, he didn't seem to mind too much. It must have been awfully nice to have a major league team think you were worth something.

Gioia felt her prospects were different. Academically, she was strong enough to get into Akron or Kent or even Walsh if she wanted, but she didn't really know what she wanted. All of her friends were talking about being doctors, or history teachers, or accountants. She didn't really want any of those things, but she didn't know what to replace them with in the conversation. With care and deliberate thought, almost as though it would make some difference in her future, she began to rearrange the pictures of long ago greats that she had printed off some website. Of course she knew that putting Bob Feller closer to the front and shifting Sandy Koufax to the left wasn't going to change anything, but then again, what could yet another new configuration hurt?

3

One of the easiest ways for Gioia to get some extra field time was to go with her father when he was doing grounds work at the ball field. He never asked her to help, though sometimes she did anyway. She liked being on a diamond; any excuse to be there was good enough for her. Plus, there was something perfectly cliche about freshly cut grass. It had a smell to it that could either be intoxicating or nauseating depending on whether or not the one doing the smelling had hay fever or particularly fond memories of summer. Gioia didn't have hay fever, so that was a point in her favor. She sat in the wire fenced dugout, sketching pine trees with a stick in the dirt as she waited for her father to finish mowing the outfield. Otherwise, the place was deserted. The girls' fields always were.

The Tusky Valley girls' softball team played down by the railroad tracks at what had once been, presumably, a very nice field. It had been a diamond for what seemed like a century. Maybe longer. Sure it developed significant puddles when it rained, which then became breeding grounds for mosquitoes all summer long, but it was a labor of love. The county parks department was always quick to remind them that girls' softball was lucky to have fields to play on at all.

Gioia glanced up from her landscape and out to the mound. She was going to have to remind her father to put new dirt out there or she was going to catch a cleat during the next game. Just as she was about to call to him, she realized that the man standing there was not her father at all. He was taller, for starters, not that Gioia would ever accuse her father of being short. She stood up and started out to the mound. That was her territory and part of her felt protective of it. "Hey, you!" She called to the man.

He smiled and tipped his hat to her. "Fine morning, Miss."

Amused by this gesture, Gioia laughed. No one had ever tipped his hat to her before. "What are you doing on my mound?" She tried to tease.

He looked back at her quizzically, almost as amused as she had been. "Yours, Miss?"

"I'm the pitcher for the Tusky Valley girls, yes." She gestured back at the scoreboard. It was more than a bit weathered and the wood was cracking in odd places, but it still plainly read, Tusky Valley Girls' Softball.

"Tusky Valley? This is Tusky Valley?" His face appeared distressed. He didn't intend to be in any place called Tusky Valley.

"The school district, yeah. This town is called Zoarville."

The distressed expression cleared from his face and it broke into an contented smile. "Close enough to home. Finally got it right. Better than Findlay anyway." He began to circle the mound.

"Where's home?" She began to ask. It was then she noticed that he was carrying a baseball.

"You say you're the pitcher?" He asked abruptly from the middle of his nostalgic revelry.

She nodded proudly. "Probably the best the Trojans have had in years."

He smirked a little. "A girl pitcher...what do you know...?"

"Don't you start. I'm better than my brother and he plays in the minors."

"Don't get huffy," he said quickly. "I remember some girls in ball in my day. Lizzie Arlington...she was all right. Second baseman, though."

"I've...never heard of her." She desperately wanted to ask this man when "his day" was. He didn't look any older than her father, but he acted like the much older men that came to the coffee shop in the mornings, mixed with a good dose of the mannerisms affected by the actors on the local vintage baseball team.

"I think I remember there being some girl pitcher. I actually think she was from around here."

"You know, I would prefer it if you just said pitcher - like any other pitcher. None of this 'girl pitcher' stuff. I'm as good as anyone else."

He smirked. "Prove it," he said, before handing her the baseball. "Show me what you can do."

Gioia took a deep breath and looked around for a target, something that would erase any doubts. She pointed toward a sign hanging on a nearby fence. It had been leftover from the last game and, while a little ragged, was still cheering the team on. "I'm going to hit the center of the o," she propositioned, knowing full well that it wouldn't be a challenge.

"Let's see how close you can get," he suggested.

She wound up and threw, hitting the center directly. A smug smile came over her face as she looked back at the man. "What do you think?" But, he was gone. Nowhere to be seen.

Mr. Rinaldi, however, had put the lawn mower away and was walking toward her. "Gioia, were you talking to yourself?" He called, sounding a little concerned.

"Of..." She was concerned as well. There was no way he could have run off so fast, absolutely no way. "Of course not."

"I think the heat's getting to you," he said with a laugh. "Come on, let's get home."

"Or the mosquitoes," she suggested. "Is hallucinating a sign of malaria?"

"Not that I know of." Mr. Rinaldi put an arm around his daughter's shoulders as they walked back to the truck. She kept looking around for that man, but there was absolutely no sign of him. It was strange. He could have hidden behind something, she supposed, but what could possibly have been the motivation?

"You didn't see anyone else around, did you?" she tried, hoping not to sound too disturbed.

Mr. Rinaldi shook his head. "You sure you're feeling well?" He reached over to touch her forehead with the back of his hand.

She jerked back a bit, resenting the insinuation. "I'm fine...really." Quickly, she tried to think of a cover story, a good change of subject. "How long has this field been here?" She attempted.

"Probably about as long as the high school, I'd guess. Maybe a little longer. I don't really know."

"It's always given off that centuries old vibe to me."

"Now, *that* might be a sign of malaria..." He teased.

Gioia shook her head. "No, no, that's just the West Nile."

4

When Marco Rinaldi went to play for the Akron Aeroes, no one in Tuscarawas County knew what to do with themselves. The local paper covered his signing with such vigor, one would have thought he was running for president. It had been quite some time since one of their boys went beyond high school ball. To say a Tusky Valley alumnus was playing professional baseball, even in the minor leagues, was incredibly impressive. Most alumni went into very normal and respectable careers like dentistry or mechanics. No one expected it would happen again for a very long time. Only five or six players in the history of baseball had gone from Tuscarawas County to the majors. The most recent was Whitney Moore in 1936. It was a once in a lifetime event.

Thanks to this, most of the high school seniors throughout the county had grown to accept the fact that very few scouts came to local games and they had all trained themselves to not even suggest this possibility to their any of their mentors. Most of all, it was never to be mentioned at the required beginning of the year meeting with the guidance counselor.

Mr. Peters' office was full of college memorabilia from so many schools, he couldn't possibly have attended them all. There were pamphlets, scholarship applications, and banners, all advertising that next big step after high school: the impending choice that would assign you to a lifetime of wishing you had made a different one. At least, that was how Gioia felt about it as she sat silently, waiting for Mr. Peters to return. She had been lucky. Her last name began with an R, so she had been able to avoid this confrontation until almost the middle of September. She had a feeling it wasn't going to go well. Taking a deep breath, she shifted her focus to the Harvard pendant hanging behind the desk.

The door opened and Mr. Peters, a heavy set man with care worn eyes and a well earned bald patch, came in. "Sorry about that," He apologized. "I hate to be late, but it was an urgent matter."

"It's all right. We can reschedule if you want...." She crossed her fingers tightly, hoping in vain that he would agree.

"No, no. I've got to get through all of you by the end of the month. We're on a tight schedule here." Gioia hoped that he meant the school was on a tight schedule with appointments. She knew well that she had until November to deal with the disappointment of applications herself.

When she didn't say anything further, Mr. Peters continued. "So, Miss Rinaldi, do you have any thoughts about college?"

"That I should go to one?" She said noncommittally.

He laughed, trying to keep the mood in the office from getting any tenser."Any one in particular?"

She shrugged. "Any one that will take me?"

Mr. Peters frowned at that. "You have good grades, Miss Rinaldi. I don't think you have to worry about that."

"Maybe I've got good grades, but I don't have a small fortune." She couldn't look him in the eye and began picking at the varnish on the chair's arm rest.

A thoughtful pause followed. Many students were very aware of that particular pitfall. It was getting harder and harder to make them ignore it. "There's always loans," he explained.

"I'm not interested in a mountain of debt either." She continued to pick at the varnish, wondering vaguely how old the chair might be.

"Scholarships then?"

She nodded, having expected that to come up eventually. "Think my grades are good enough?"

"Perhaps." His voice was so optimistic it irritated her.

She looked up. It was now or never. If she was going to ask the question she wanted to ask more than anything, she had to ask it now. "What about ball?"

He paused again, looking stunned this time. Usually by now, students had written off such pie-in-the-sky hopes. "You would need a Division One school for a scholarship like that."

"You don't think I'm good enough for a Division One school?"

He shook his head, trying to think of a tactful way to word such a letdown."I think it's hard to get a Division One school to look at our students."

"My brother..." She began.

Frustrated with the fact that she was pushing an issue that most others, even the boys, left alone, Mr.

Peters couldn't help exclaiming, "You're going to make me say it?!"

Gioia wasn't surprised by the outburst. She simply shook her head, a bit resigned. "I suppose not." She knew he would tell her that her brother was different. He drew a crowd to the Tusky Valley games just to watch him play. He would tell her that it didn't matter how talented she was, the girls' games didn't draw a crowd. They couldn't get scouts if they didn't draw a crowd.

"Do you want me to select a few other ones for you?" He asked then in a much more sympathetic voice. He felt deeply guilty for snapping at a student. Disappointing the students like that was not what he had become a counselor to do.

She shrugged and went back to her efforts with the varnish.

"What are your interests?" He asked. "What do you want to study?"

She shrugged again.

"Besides baseball, I mean," He tried to tease.

Gioia frowned. She had thought about it, but she hadn't really come to any particular conclusion. She liked economics well enough and science to some degree, but it just didn't come close to the rush of playing a good game. "I...guess I don't know..."

Mr. Peters got up and flipped through a few pamphlets. "Sports Management?...No, that's very male dominated...but there's sports medicine? Journalism?"

She bristled at his quick dismissal of sports management as a possible career choice. "I don't know."

"Miss Rinaldi, it's your senior year. You have things that you need to be thinking about."

She protested immediately, his assumptions were growing increasingly irritating. "I am thinking about them."

"I don't think you're thinking hard enough." His voice was pleading.

She stood up from the chair. "I think we're done talking for now."

"Miss Rinaldi, this is for your own good."

"I know." She shook her head and started out of the room.

"We'll meet again." When she didn't respond, he shook his head and made a few notes in her file.

After effectively storming out of the office, Gioia made her way to the library for study hall and took a seat with a sigh. The blonde she had sat across from looked up with a smirk. "Where have you been?" the girl asked.

"Meeting with Peters." Gioia said as she opened her math textbook and took out a half finished problem set.

"How'd that go?"

"About as well as I expected."

"Rinaldi! Dessecker!" a brusk voice shouted from the front of the room. "This is a study hall!"

The two girls looked embarrassed and dropped their heads, trying to cover their snickers. Nellie ripped a piece of paper from her notebook and scribbled on it:

He decide where you get to go to college?

Gioia shook her head and took out her own piece, writing:

We didn't get that far.

?

I told him I wanted to get a softball scholarship.

?

I do.

What did he say?

I wasn't thinking hard enough.

Nellie paused a long moment before she wrote anything further. She didn't want to offend her friend, but she felt Mr. Peters was probably right. Still, she decided it was best not to go there. With Gioia that was a dangerous road. Instead of what she really wanted to say, she wrote:

He told me I wasn't smart enough for college.

Gioia looked up at her, puzzled, and shook her head. Nellie was smart. That was a silly thing to say. With a quick glance back at the study hall supervisor, she continued writing.

No.

He did. My ACT scores aren't so high.

That's all?

That's what colleges care about.

That's not true.

Nellie rolled her eyes. "I'm not taking advice from a seventeen year old who still wants to be a baseball player when she grows up," she muttered to herself.

"Thanks." Gioia said bitterly as she crumpled up her note paper and jammed it into her bag.

Nellie sighed. She hadn't meant to offend. Trying to draw her friend back into conversation and soothe hurt feelings she wrote:

Its not your fault that it's unrealistic.

As Gioia read the words, she nodded slowly, but it was a noncommittal nod. It wasn't her fault, still...it was what she wanted. "We're allowed to have dreams," she hissed across the table.

Rolling her eyes in the direction of the study hall supervisor, Nellie continued to write.

I know that, but

"No." Gioia stood up from the table and started toward the book shelves, if for no other reason than that destination meant that the study hall supervisor couldn't yell at her for getting up from her seat.

The school library's stacks were a touch on the limited side and they hadn't been weeded recently, but budgets were tight and the school did its best. If nothing else they were able to have a few duplicate textbooks, some browse-able fiction which even included some quality contemporary books along with the classics, and a decent section on local history. Gioia selected a book from the shelf at random and opened it to the middle. She just needed to stand there long enough for the supervisor to think she actually had a reason for getting up.

On the pages before her under the fancy old-fashioned typeface scrawl of "Tuscarawas County's Most Famous Son" was an image of the man she was speaking to yesterday. "That's impossible," she muttered to herself. Though why she hadn't noticed the resemblance before, she couldn't imagine. Maybe it was his grandson.

"What's impossible?" She heard Nellie asking her suddenly.

"...nothing." She shut the book carefully and put it under her arm.

"Look...I'm sorry. I didn't mean to upset you."

"Well, you did," Gioia replied bitterly.

"Can you forgive me?"

Gioia pretended to think about it for awhile. "I suppose I could always get a new best friend. I could hold auditions or something."

Nellie rolled her eyes. "Will those auditions involve pretending to be interested when you talk about some guy we'll never meet's batting average?"

"Of course, they will. That's a crucial requirement."

"Good thing I'm still around then," Nellie said with a quiet laugh. "Now, are you going to show me what you were looking at?"

"You'll think I'm silly."

"Not any more than usual."

With a look around, Gioia opened the book again to the page. "Tuscarawas County's Most Famous Son," she read in a somewhat amused voice.

"I would hate to be the child of a county," Nellie said, looking it over. "I imagine it'd be tough to get attention."

"Well..." Gioia began to explain, but Nellie hadn't yet finished her diatribe.

"Of course it's some baseball player. You going to show that to Peters? 1890s might be reaching. Don't you think?"

"He's not just -any- baseball player," Gioia protested. "He's the most famous pitcher in all of baseball history."

"Bob Feller?"

That wasn't the answer she was looking for, but Gioia couldn't help but smile. "I'm impressed that you know of him."

"I listen to you and my dad sometimes," Nellie replied, faking offense. "I know a thing or two."

"Well, that's not him. Bob Feller was born in Iowa, not Ohio...and played in a completely different time period....but, otherwise, decent guess."

Nellie grabbed the book from her friend and looked it over with a smirk. "Oh! Cy Young...nice going T-County."

"That's what I was thinking."

"So, what's the plan though? Show this book to Peters and convince him there's some magical potion in our water that makes everyone from here a super special awesome pitcher?"

Gioia grabbed the book back roughly. "Not even close."

"Then what?"

She wasn't about to tell anyone that she thought she had seen this guy hanging around the softball field. Clearly, Nellie already thought she was losing her grip on reality. It was probably a smart idea not to further add to that impression. "I have more research to do." She closed the book and started back to her seat. Nellie waited a few minutes before following.

After the final bell, Gioia made her way across the street and over to the softball field. In a haze of thought, she walked carefully around the perimeter of the field, letting her hand drag along the fence. It was completely crazy. The things her mind was saying couldn't possibly be true. As many times as she attempted to tell herself it had to be his grandson, she couldn't shake the fact that he looked so similar to the man in the picture. It wasn't just a family resemblance sort of similar; it was a same person sort of similar. Even so, the book gave the indisputable fact that he had died in 1955. Even if that weren't true, he would certainly have to have aged. None of it made any sense. Why would the ghost of Cy Young be at the Tusky Valley softball field? And, besides, there was no such thing as ghosts.

"Mr. Young?" She asked, making her way inside and onto the field and feeling incredibly absurd while doing so. "Mr. Young are you here?"

The field was empty. She knew it would be. Fall ball practice wasn't going to start for another hour. There had to be enough time for everyone to get changed and ready before heading over to the field. Still, Gioia worried that if anyone heard her they would think she lost her mind. "Mr. Young?"

"Who's Mr. Young?" asked a voice from the fence.

In a panic, Gioia spun around to see Mrs. Yoder, the softball coach, exactly the person she didn't want to see as she was calling for ghosts. If Coach Yoder thought she was having a nervous breakdown, there could be unpleasant consequences. Gioia shook her head. "No one."

"No one, huh?" Coach Yoder said, shaking her head as well. "You're not exactly a great liar, Gioia."

"Well..."

"And you're not in your practice clothes yet? Don't tell me you're sitting out tonight. We've got a game against Triway tomorrow. I need a pitcher."

"No...I know...I was just going to change..."

"Were you?" Gioia nodded quickly, but Coach Yoder raised a skeptical eyebrow. "Who's Mr. Young, Gioia?"

She sighed, trying to think fast. "My brother....he...implied that there might be a scout at practice today," she lied as quickly as possible.

Coach Yoder raised an eyebrow at that. "A scout?" That was certainly a rarity. "Your brother mentioned this?"

Gioia nodded. She hated lying, but she hated even more having to tell the truth right now.

"Is he here?"

"I don't see him." That was honest enough. He had disappeared so fast the other day though, it didn't mean much.

"You don't think your brother..."

"You're probably right," she said quickly, latching on to the idea as an escape. "He was probably playing a trick on me." She scurried off the field to change into her practice clothes before Coach Yoder could comment any further or acknowledge her abrupt change of heart.

Practice went well and as expected no scouts ever showed. Coach Yoder didn't mention this to Gioia, though. She figured the girl didn't need any further ridicule on top of her brother playing pranks on her. At the end of the evening, Jennifer, another of the girls' players, sprinted in from the outfield. "Why was Coach Yoder looking at the stands all night?" she asked of Gioia and a few others who were still standing near the dugout.

All of the girls shrugged, including Gioia, though she knew the answer. As they filed out, she cast a wary glance back at the empty stands as well and saw him sitting there, baseball in hand, looking terribly pleased with himself.

"Oh no, you don't," she muttered under her breath as she stormed over to him. "You do not get to make me look like a fool."

He stood up and took off his cap as she approached. "Why if it isn't Tusky Valley's star pitcher..."

"Who -are- you?" She asked in a forceful voice.

"I'm sorry...?"

"If you're going to watch our practice I have a right to know who you are."

He nodded slowly. "I suppose you do...."

"I should call the police."

"That probably wouldn't be very effective." He repositioned his hat. "But you are welcome to try."

She considered this a moment and took a deep breath. "It...wouldn't be very effective because...?"

"That would be because no one else can see me." His words were far more matter-of-fact than Gioia would have expected that sort of statement to sound.

"No one else can see you?"

He nodded. "I suppose I'm what they'd call a spirit or a ghost."

Gioia looked at him and shook her head immediately. "I don't believe in ghosts. There's no such thing."

"And yet here I am."

A long pause followed. Gioia didn't quite know what to say after that. All she knew was that she had absolutely no idea what was happening. "Who are you the ghost of?"

He shrugged. "Does that matter?"

"Of course it matters." She took a few steps down the stands, quite frustrated, but then turned back with a smirk. "I'm pretty sure I've already got a good idea either way."

"You're probably wrong."

"I'm probably not."

"It's been a -long- time since I played, a very long time. I doubt I'm the person you'd expect."

"Are you implying I don't know my baseball history?"

He shook his head apologetically. "Not at all. You misunderstand me..."

"1890s, right?"

He nodded, finally, looking impressed. "Doing your research?"

Gioia didn't answer. She wasn't going to say what she had discovered accidentally, not yet anyway. She just smirked. "I need to get home. Enjoy the mosquitoes."

"They're not so bad when you have no blood," he said in a mocking voice.

"I imagine not." She walked down the rest of the bleachers and hurried away. What she had just experienced made absolutely no sense. There was no such thing as ghosts, but there he was: a ghost, an honest to goodness baseball ghost. It was a little too much to take.

5

When Gioia got home that evening the kitchen was a floury mess. "Madre?" She asked when she opened the door and was assaulted by the cloud of white dust. "What's going on?"

A laugh came from somewhere in the fog. "I wanted to bake some bread," her mother's melodic voice rang out.

"Where are you?" Gioia asked, pushing through it.

"It'll settle. Just wait a minute."

"Where am I supposed to do my homework?"

"It'll settle."

Gioia set her bag down near the door and maneuvered her way through the crowded little kitchen to open the window. "Maybe this will help." Slowly the flour in the air began to dissipate and forms became clearer. Her mother was standing over the table, hair and clothes absolutely covered in flour. She didn't seem to care. A slab of dough lay on wax paper in front of her and that was all that mattered. She was smiling.

"Hungry?" She asked.

Gioia nodded. "Anything other than bread?"

"I can make you a sandwich." She took a fresh loaf and began cutting slices. "Spinach and Red Peppers? Mozzarella?"

"Yes. To all of that." Gioia cleared a space on the table and took out her books, hoping her teachers wouldn't mind a dusting of flour on her work. Watching her mother cook was inspiring. She had such a zeal for food, preparing each of the ingredients with relish and care. She cut the peppers like she was liberating them and held each ball of mozzarella like they were tiny hearts ready for transplant. To see someone care so much for their craft, even if it was just a sandwich, was simply marvelous.

"So how was school?" She asked as she pressed the sandwich.

Gioia shrugged. "Not too eventful."

"Really? Not eventful?" She took the sandwich, placed it on a plate and presented it to her daughter as though it were a priceless jewel.

Gioia shook her head, noticing the absolutely perfect tiny grill marks. How her mother managed such things, she could only guess. "I met with Mr. Peters. That's pretty much it."

"Ah, Peters...how's he doing these days?"

"We didn't really get around to talking about his personal life." She took a bite of the sandwich. Exquisite.

"Fair enough. Did you discuss college at all?"

"Not in any sort of productive way. He mostly just scoffed a lot."

Mrs. Rinaldi sighed. "And can you really blame him, Gioia?"

"Madre!"

"He sees this every single day: these kids with big dreams. It's a tough world out there. Sometimes...they don't get what they want." She look wistfully toward the window a moment. Then as quickly as the melancholy came on, she shook her head and rushed over to the oven, pulling out a tray of fresh loaves.

"I'm not really the kind of girl that..."

Mrs. Rinaldi set the tray down on the counter with a loud clang. "No one thinks they're the kind of person that defers their dreams, until they've become that person."

This conversation really wasn't sitting well with Gioia. Her mother sounded so pessimistic, which was not her usual attitude, particularly when she was in the kitchen. "Madre...I..."

"I know we don't talk much about the big bad future, Gioia, but..." she paused, looking incredibly unsure of how to continue the thought in her head without perhaps sounding offensive. "I only want you to be happy." It didn't seem like that was what she actually wanted to say.

"I think I will be."

She took a deep breath and continued. "We don't have a lot of money." That was closer to the truth. Gioia could tell by the resigned tone in her mother's voice. She absolutely despised talking about this sort of thing. Reality was troublesome.

"I told Mr. Peters that. I'm well aware."

"You didn't have to tell Mr. Peters." She looked slightly embarrassed, as though half the county wasn't in the same boat.

"It's his job to help me find scholarships, Madre. He offered."

"I know that, but..."

"Not like he was much help."

"Gioia." She sat down next to her daughter at the table. "I don't want you to think that you don't deserve everything..."

Gioia merely raised an eyebrow, continuing to finish her dinner. Where was this going?

"You do, Gioia. You do deserve everything. You are smart and strong and...strong willed. You've got ambition, which is half the battle sometimes, believe you me."

"Madre..." She was starting to grow more certain that she didn't want to hear this.

"I'm just saying...sometimes the world doesn't give you what you deserve. Sometimes not even close."

Gioia didn't know what to say. She nodded slowly and carefully. All the words she formed seemed to feel dry and failed to produce themselves. Finally, she managed to force out, "I'm a hard worker."

"I would never say you weren't."

"Doesn't that..."

"It helps. Sometimes. But it's not always enough." She looked back to the window again, but as before she immediately shook her head.

"Is something wrong, Madre?"

"Of course not. What could possibly be wrong?" She took her daughter's hand in hers and squeezed it. "Every night I pray, my joyous girl, that you will find what you're supposed to do. I know there's something."

"Thanks, Madre." She didn't know what else to say. Her mother was not typically a maudlin woman. She had always had a sad sort of elegance about her that made her look like a silent film star with her wide eyes conveying perhaps something of a false naivety and dark hair cropped into a very practical and yet glamorous Louise Brooks style bob. It was a beauty that Gioia and many of her friends wished from time to time that they could achieve. Still, the sadness never actually seemed to come from her attitude toward life. It was a distressing change. Something had to have happened. Something she wasn't saying. It was a bit much for Gioia at the moment. "Madre, can...might I be able to take my work upstairs to my room."

She nodded and spoke quite quietly, letting go of her hand. "Of course, darling."

Gioia slipped out of the kitchen and cast a worried glance back at her mother as she did so. She had to talk to Marco soon. Maybe he knew something.

She waited until later that night to call him, wanting to make sure he was actually available to talk. He answered sounding very tired, but far less irritated than he did back when she had once, accidentally, called him during a class. "Hello?" he asked sounding half asleep.

"I'm sorry did I wake you?"

"Gioia?" He sounded quite surprised to be hearing from his sister. "What time is it?"

She glanced at the clock. It was only midnight. "Not late enough for you to be asleep. Don't you have studying to do? Or a party to be at?"

"Why are you calling me?"

"I don't..." she trailed off unsure of how to word her question now that she actually had her brother on the other line. "It's Madre..."

Any trace of irritation was suddenly gone from his voice. "Is something wrong?"

"That's what I was calling to ask you."

He sighed, sounding as if he were trying to wake up his mind. "Why?"

"I don't know. Today she was just...she sounded so...sad."

"She always sounds sad."

"No, she doesn't," Gioia protested. She was a dreamer. She wasn't sad.

"Gioia, have you met our mother?"

"She's imaginative. She's whimsical..."

"She's sad." Marco was getting aggravated now. His tone was dismissive and annoyed.

"Why?" It sounded like such a bizarre question.

"I don't know. She just is. Always has been. I think it's one of those adulthood things. Midlife crisis or something."

"She's never struck me as sad."

"Gioia, I'm tired. I have practice in the morning and classes. I don't really want to argue with you about this. Unless something has actually happened…"

Gioia shook her head and puzzled over her conversation with her mother a moment. "Fine, I…I just called to see if maybe something had happened. They always tell you things…"

"I know nothing you don't know."

"Are you sure?"

"Yes," he replied so loudly that Gioia had to move the phone away from her ear for a moment.

She took a deep breath before trying again. She didn't want him to start thinking of her as some stereotypically annoying little sister, but she knew he always knew about family matters first. Her parents far too often tried to shield her from seeing their hardships. "They told you when the bank was trying to take the house."

"That was years ago. You were too small to understand. You're old enough now. They'd tell you."

"Are you absolutely sure?"

"Absolutely. Now can I go to sleep?"

With another sigh, Gioia nodded, but then remembering her brother couldn't hear that through the phone, she sighed yet again. "Yeah, sure. Sorry to bother you." She hung up the phone before Marco could tell her to cheer up.

6

Early Saturday morning, before dawn even broke, Gioia went back down to the ball field. She didn't know what she expected to find when she got there, but she was actually quite pleased with what she found: an empty field, the grass still dewy, a nighttime chill managing to cling to the air. The mosquitoes were also much less bothersome in the morning.

She threw the ball up into the air, raced out beneath and caught it. It was nice to get moving without anyone else to bother her. She went to the mound then and took her place. Closing her eyes, she could almost hear the cheers, not just the cheers of the small town crowds, but something more. The voices of thousands rang through her ears. She moved her arm back and released the ball. It flew like a rocket over the plate. There was no one there to catch it, but she opened her eyes and smiled. The feeling was unmatchable. "Perfect."

Then came the voice. "You've got speed, no doubt about that."

She spun around quickly to see the man from the other day, standing there with arms crossed and an appraising look on his face. Her eyes were wide. "You again?"

"In my day, we didn't worry so much about speed," he said. "I mean, it was a concern, but it wasn't everything."

She frowned. "In my day, you have to have a 100 mile per hour fastball before anyone will even look at you."

"Someone's going to look at you, Joy?"

She narrowed her eyes, uncertain how she felt about him using the English version of her name, or in fact, how she felt about him knowing her name at all. "Not very inspiring for a ghost."

"Well, you are a girl...."

Gioia rolled her eyes. Not this nonsense again. "I hadn't noticed."

"Girl ball players..." he began, but Gioia didn't want to hear it. If she was going to be having hallucinations, she didn't want them to be sexist hallucinations.

"Jackie Mitchell struck out Babe Ruth and Lou Gehrig," she said quickly. She was always able to silence her brother with that particular tidbit.

The ghost seemed to ponder this a moment. "Very impressive and how recently was that?"

"I could do it too," She said with a proud smirk, rather than answering. "Do you know them? Bring them by and we'll find out what girl ball players can do."

He didn't acknowledge her dare and simply replied, "Not with that fastball you won't. You have no control."

"Excuse me?" It was incredibly flattering to be getting pitching advice from none other than Cy Young, but she still didn't appreciate having her abilities questioned.

"I bet you pitch a lot of balls."

"You...you have to keep them guessing," she said meekly, attempting to defend herself without actually admitting that it was true. "One time, I let a girl foul twice...."

"Let...?"

Gioia narrowed her eyes "I let her foul twice, then followed with three intentional balls, but that I threw the fourth one...right down the middle. She didn't even swing at it."

The ghost did not appear impressed. "That's a cheap trick."

"It certainly got the job done."

"It's not seemly for a young lady to be so arrogant."

She scoffed at that. She didn't dare be anything other than arrogant when it came to athletics. Confidence was key. "Maybe not in the 1890s."

"Joy..."

She still wasn't sure that she liked being called that. "Look, to get what I want, I can't just be good. I have to be the best. And not only that, I have to think I'm the best. You slip up for a second, show even an ounce of weakness and you give them an in to picking you apart."

"And what is that? What is it that you want?"

She looked at him seriously, considering for a moment how much she could trust the products of her own imagination. "I'm going to tell you secret."

The ghost nodded, looking at her with a quizzical, expectant expression.

"I want to play professional baseball," she admitted. "It's the only thing I want to do. I really, really want to play in the major leagues, the real major leagues."

He smiled bemused, but remained silent.

She went on. "I know you don't think it's possible. No one does, but I'm twice as good as my brother and ten times more passionate about the game. It's everything to me."

"I can see that," he said finally.

"If I...am the best there is..." she struggled a little to explain. Most people figured she just wanted to play softball in college, if they only knew the rest, they would never let her live it down. None of that changed how much she wanted it, however. "If I am the best there is and I work harder than anyone else..."

"You're willing to do that?" he asked seriously.

"I'm willing to do whatever it takes."

A long silence followed. Gioia felt a familiar pit in her stomach. It was the same one that plagued her when boys found out that she played or that she knew more statistics than they did. People always looked at her different. It hurt, the way they looked at her. She hated it. The silence was enough for Gioia to assume for a moment that her new friend had gone. Then, just as she was about to go collect the ball, he spoke. "Then perhaps I can work with you after all."

"What's that supposed to mean?" She asked suspiciously.

Before she knew it the ball was back in her glove and the gentleman was standing behind home plate. "Go on, throw it."

"You going to catch without gear?" She smirked. "You saw how fast I can throw."

"I seriously doubt that it's going to hurt me."

Gioia laughed at that. "No. I suppose not." She threw the ball with the greatest speed she could muster.

He caught it barehanded with ease. "The way these balls are manufactured, that would have been a double at least, if someone hit it."

"No way," she protested defensively.

"I'm not trying to take away from your natural talent. You've got that in spades."

"Yes, you are. You're trying to say I'm not good enough."

"You really can't be so defensive when people are just trying to help you."

"I have to be. I have to assume that people are out to get me because subconsciously, they are."

He rolled his eyes, but didn't comment. "Throw again. Try to make it a strike this time." Out of nowhere, he was standing with a bat.

That came as quite a shock. She wasn't entirely sure how to respond. "Let me finish warming up first," she managed to force out after a moment.

With a flash, the bat was gone. "Just let me know when you're ready."

Gioia took a deep breath. She stretched. She paced. She tried to clear her head. He waited patiently at the plate as though he had all the time in the world. "All right!" she called. "I'm going to throw now."

The bat appeared yet again. "Take your best shot."

She did just as he asked, and wished Coach Yoder had been standing there with her radar. She could feel the speed when she released it. Unfortunately, despite the speed, the ball was right down the middle and the bat connected perfectly. She grimaced when she heard the crack. How she hated that sound.

"See what I mean?" the ghost asked, not running, merely standing there at home plate looking vindicated.

"Yes, yes, I see what you mean," she muttered. "Should have thrown a curve, but then I would have proven you right."

"How so?" He asked, an eyebrow raised.

"My curveballs..." she trailed off, trying to think of the least incriminating way to explain. "They tend to get a little wild."

"That's what we're going to work on."

"Is it now?" she asked skeptically. "Listen, I'm flattered that you've decided to be my new pitching coach and all, but..."

"But?"

"I..." She couldn't think of the proper way to say what she was thinking. She was truly worried she had lost her mind. "I don't believe in ghosts."

"You don't believe in ghosts?" He was no longer at home plate, but standing right next to her.

"No. I watch horror movies all the time. They never scare me."

He nodded slowly. "Then...what do you suppose is happening right now?"

"My mind can't cope with the fact that I have to go to college. I've invented a defense mechanism." She smiled at that. Her psychology teacher would be very proud.

"Is that so?"

"Makes more sense than the ghost of Cy Young appearing at Tusky Valley High School."

An impressed expression again showed itself. She knew who he was. "Well, I'm from the southern end of Tuscarawas County, for a start, and call me Cyclone. Everybody does."

"No." She refused plainly.

"All right...then my real name's Denton...."

"I don't mean that. I meant-"

"Look," he interrupted. "Maybe you are hallucinating. Maybe you're not. Either way, I'm offering to help you with your pitching. You can take me up on it or not, but I'm offering. If you want to be great, you need a great coach."

"I have -"

"And she's a lovely woman, I'm sure, but does she have a pitching award named after her?"

Gioia had to concede that particular fact. "What do you want me to do?"

"Meet me here, every Saturday morning. I don't care how cold it is, but stick with it and by spring you'll have every college you can imagine recruiting you."

It sounded lovely, but Gioia was doubtful. "Only Division One schools give sports scholarships."

"You'll have plenty of those."

"And applications start coming due in November."

"Then we better hurry. Just meet me here, every Saturday. Can you commit to that?"

If her hallucinations were willing to promise college scholarships, giving up Saturday mornings seemed like a very simple sacrifice. "Absolutely."

And so she did. Every Saturday morning, she got up early and went down to the ball field and met with Cyclone, as he preferred to be called. He explained to her that the most important things about pitching, to him anyway, were focus and control. "It doesn't matter how fast your fastball is or what kind of curve you've got if it goes all over the place," he would say at least once a practice.

Gioia would roll her eyes every single time, but she did try to take his advice to heart. She'd read it in countless books before, but somehow it felt different coming from the man himself. A few times she was tempted to ask if there were any other baseball ghosts that could lend a hand, but she stopped herself. It sounded a bit on the greedy side.

At practice, Coach Yoder watched Gioia carefully. Something was different about her. She seemed more focused, a little less desperate. "Miss Rinaldi!" She called at the end of practice one day as the girls started filing to their water bottles.

Gioia was right over. "Yes, coach?"

"You've been working on your curveball?" she asked curiously.

"On everything, actually."

Coach Yoder considered this a moment "With your brother?"

Gioia shook her head. "No, ma'am."

Trying not to appear disappointed that she wasn't using the county's best known star, Coach Yoder nodded. "Good. You know that baseball is different than softball."

"I'm aware of that, Coach Yoder."

"Good. Well, keep up your good work. I like what I'm seeing."

Gioia nodded as well, feeling proud but trying not to look it. "Yes ma'am." As Coach Yoder walked away, Gioia glanced over at the grove of trees. Cy wasn't there, but she felt grateful all the same. She liked the feeling of accomplishment that she had now. It felt like things were coming together. Even if they weren't.

7

Tusky Valley High School was abuzz with a great deal of sports gossip that October. Football was doing quite well that season; Homecoming was coming up, and not to mention a few people were even starting to notice that the girl's fall ball team was undefeated. When the next game was mentioned on the morning announcements, a general muttering of confusion came over Gioia's homeroom class. "I didn't even know we had fall softball," one of the boys muttered to a friend.

"Neither did I," his friend replied.

A couple of them even glanced over at Gioia. "You're the pitcher right?" the first boy asked.

"Yes," she said, grinning proudly. She knew as far as school's sports hierarchy went girls' softball ranked just above scholar challenge, but she didn't realize so few people even knew they had a team at all.

"Are you any good?" asked another, his voice clearly mocking.

Gioia didn't care. She nodded, feeling a bit smug over this season's accomplishments. "We're undefeated, what do you think?"

"How hard can it be to beat a bunch of girls?" The whole group laughed, even other girls in the classroom.

That comment caught her a bit off guard. "I...I don't really think that makes much of a difference."

Jennifer, the left fielder, was also in Gioia's homeroom and came to her defense. "I bet we could beat the boy's baseball team too," she said sounding rather even tempered, though Gioia couldn't imagine how.

Since she was relatively popular, the class seemed to quiet a little. "You tell Carson that?" a boy in the front of the room asked. Gioia remembered his name: Jason. He used to point at laugh at her in elementary school. Her father said it was because he thought she was pretty. She thought that was inaccurate at the time and thought doubly so now. There was nothing attractive about being mocked.

Jennifer just smirked. Her boyfriend, Carson Vand, was a linebacker on the football team and one of the school's more popular boys. The social standing meant she could get away with more. "He's well aware."

Gioia jumped back into the argument, her temper and age old irritation with Jason getting the better of her. "And besides I don't think who her boyfriend is has anything to do with whether or not we're good ball players."

"Oooo..." several of the students said in unison. One of them even whistled.

"No wonder Carson doesn't care," another of the boys said in a loud fake whisper.

Jason laughed. "I bet he really likes it. Always wondered why you had pictures of softball players in your locker, Gioia."

Jennifer looked irritated but remained in her seat. Gioia wasn't going to tolerate it. "Shut up," she said, standing.

There were a few more whistles. "Go on you two, give us a kiss," Jason continued to push. "Show us why Carson approves."

"If you don't shut up, my fist is going to kiss you," Gioia said angrily. Jennifer just rolled her eyes and pretended to ignore them.

"Miss Rinaldi, please sit down," the homeroom teacher interrupted finally.

"But...Mrs. Jones," Gioia protested, irritated that she hadn't bothered to interrupt the taunting prior to now.

"Sit down or I'm sending you to Mr. Peters' office."

Gioia's head was spinning. She was so irritated, she didn't know how to respond. For a few precious moments, she thought her talents were going to be, for once, acknowledged, but that turned out to not be the case. She almost wanted to be sent to Mr. Peters' office. It was better than being in the classroom right now. She shook her head and didn't sit down.

"All right, Miss Rinaldi," Mrs. Jones said with an aggravated sigh as she handed her a hall pass. "Go on."

Without a word, Gioia quickly left the room. She could have sworn she heard another whistle as she closed the door behind her. Tears welled up in her eyes for reasons she didn't quite understand as she hurried down the hall.

Mr. Peters had been hoping to have Gioia back into the office again before November when college application season began, but he had not been expecting her to come to the office of her own accord. He looked up in surprise when she knocked at the door of his office. He always left it open for the students unless he was in a meeting. "Miss Rinaldi?" He asked rather startled. He could see that her eyes were red. "Homeroom isn't over yet, is it?"

"Mrs. Jones sent me down to see you," she said with a shrug, waving the hall pass. Her anger had dissipated a little. Now she just felt a bit hollow.

"Oh...and why'd she do that?" He asked, very concerned, gesturing toward the chair in front of his desk.

Gioia shrugged, still standing in the doorway. "Maybe I'll just go."

"No, please, take a seat." She obliged and he got up to close the door. "What seems to be troubling you?"

She shrugged yet again. "It's silly..."

"Is it nerves about college? That's completely normal."

"No I..." To be honest she hadn't given much thought to college lately except for her ghost Cy's promise to ensure that scouts from every college imaginable would be recruiting her. It hadn't happened yet, but he assured her it would. There was still time.

"Family trouble?"

"No...family stuff's great. They're always great. I'm lucky..." She trailed off, unsure of how to go on.

"Miss Rinaldi..." He felt a sense of worry overcoming him. Whenever students came in to his office on their own, but were evasive like this, it usually meant that something quite serious was bothering them.

"I..." she looked to the floor and took a deep breath. "I threatened some boy in my class."

He had not been expecting that, and it was impossible to hide the shock in his tone. "Gioia...why would you do something like that?"

"They were making fun of me. Practically the whole class was making fun of me and Jennifer and Mrs. Jones just ignored them." She felt the indignation rising up in her again.

"Making fun?" He asked with care, trying to get to the root of the problem.

"Teasing, really...me and Jennifer...about softball. It's silly. I shouldn't have...I should have just..."

Mr. Peters took a deep breath. "No, you shouldn't have threatened him; however, he shouldn't have been teasing you."

She felt a little vindicated at that. "That's what I was thinking."

"Can you tell me his name?"

She shook her head. "I don't want to be that person, Mr. Peters."

"I'm not going to give him a detention or anything. He won't even know you told me."

"Then why bother?"

"I just want to keep an eye out."

Gioia thought about it for a long while. She didn't want to, but since she wasn't allowed to hit him maybe having Mr. Peters keep an eye out was the next best thing for the moment. "Jason Becker," she said quietly. "He was...he wasn't the only one...they were all laughing and whistling...it's just..."

"Whistling?"

She shook her head. "He's the one who said...he started..."she trailed off. It had been such a small thing. Jason had probably already forgotten that he'd said it. Why was it tugging at her mind so?

"What did he say, Gioia?"

"...give us a kiss..." she said in a dry, flat whisper, wanting immediately to sink into a puddle on the floor.

Mr. Peters frowned and nodded slowly. "I'll keep an eye on him." He wanted to say more. He wanted to say a lot more; however, the school didn't quite have a policy on this.

"Thank you." She started to stand up.

"While I have you here, Miss Rinaldi..."

She stopped and sank back down in the chair with a sigh. "No, I don't know about college yet," she said somewhat bitterly. "And I don't really feel like talking about it right now."

"Thanksgiving's coming up fast. Most schools like to have your applications right around then."

"I know. Believe me, I know."

"Then you need to make a few decisions." He stood up and pulled out her file. From it he took a pile of brochures, which he handed to her. "I've gathered a few ideas for you."

Gioia skimmed the tops of the brochures. It was an interesting range, smaller schools like Mount Union and Marietta to much bigger schools like Bowling Green.

"Options..." she said uncertainly.

"I've looked it all over as best I can and they all seem to have decent softball teams."

"And how much do they cost?"

"You can't limit yourself by that," Mr. Peters replied, sounding frustrated.

"Why can't I?" The anger was coming back and she felt defiant. She wanted to know what it was going to take to make him understand?

"Because you're a smart talented girl..."

"That's not enough!" She couldn't stop herself from shouting.

"If you look in there, there's also a list of academic scholarships that I think are within your reach."

"Within my reach..." she muttered. It sounded a bit like a damning condemnation of her academic abilities.

"You know what I mean, Miss Rinaldi."

She continued to flip through to the list. "I'll look into it."

"Just what I was hoping to hear." That statement was something of a lie. He had been hoping to hear that she had already decided and filled out three applications and that he didn't need to give her the information he had gathered, but at least finally getting her to agree to look into it was a start.

"I'll look into it," she repeated.

"Good. I think we should meet again next week to discuss this."

"Sure, next week." At this point she would say anything to get out of his office. "Can I go now?"

"Of course, Miss Rinaldi," he said. She left as quickly as she could.

8

Back at home, Gioia sat at the table, examining the brochures that Mr. Peters had given her. It still felt so incredibly overwhelming. How was she supposed to choose her future right now? She was only seventeen. Everyone was constantly telling her that she was too young to be making serious decisions. Weren't college and potential careers serious decisions?

Mount Union looked like it had a decent sports program, but it was quite expensive. Bowling Green was cheaper, but still not cheap enough. Nothing was cheap enough. Not by a long shot. She would have to get a scholarship of some kind.

"What's all this?" Came a voice from the doorway.

Gioia turned around to see her father standing there and shook her head. "Nothing..."

"Nothing takes up the whole kitchen table?"

"Nothing important."

He walked over and picked up one of the brochures. "Oh, college isn't important now?"

Gioia shook her head. "Mr. Peters gave all this to me. I told him I'd at least look at it."

"And so you are." He sat down in a chair next to her and started looking at one for Akron. "You've seen Akron a few times. You like it, don't you?"

"I do..." she replied noncommittally.

"And your brother goes there. He can keep an eye on you."

She shrugged. "I suppose. I don't think he'd like that much though...little sister, cramping his style..."

"Nonsense," he said, actually sounding jovial. "Marco adores you. If my sisters and I had the kind of relationship that you two do..."

"College is different."

"Maybe we can get some kind of 'two kids go there' discount?" He mused, still examining the Akron University brochure.

That got Gioia's attention. "They can do that?"

"We can look into it." He passed the brochure over to Gioia and she looked at it, actually seeing it this time.

"Maybe next time we visit Marco?" She suggested. "Maybe we could stop real quick in the office...?"

"Have you decided what you want to major in?" Her father ventured, knowing full well that this was dangerous territory.

Gioia's frown returned. That question made all the good feelings about choosing a school vanish. "No..."

Her father shook his head at that. "No? Whatever happened to economics?"

"I like economics," she replied, still unsure.

"It sounds like a good major, and lot of people seem to know very little about it..." He laughed, trying to cover the nervousness in his voice. "I know I certainly don't."

"I like it well enough, I just don't know if I want to be an economist."

"Why not?"

"There's...other things I'd rather be."

"Like?" His voice gave away that he already knew the answer.

Gioia wasn't sure that she wanted to answer him. She was pretty sure she knew what he would say and she didn't want to have to hear it. Still, she had always trusted her father and wanted to be as open with him as possible. "Baseball," she replied honestly. "...I want to be a pitcher."

He nodded. That was exactly what he had thought she would say. "You can certainly play ball in college."

"No, I mean...I want to be a pitcher for my career. I want to be a professional pitcher." Once she had started, she realized that the word were just spilling out of her mouth like she had sprung a leek. "There's nothing else in the world that makes me as happy as baseball, Padre. Absolutely nothing. Nothing. I want to play..." With great effort, she managed to stop herself, realizing that she was rambling.

"Gioia..." he began.

"Marco plays."

"Marco is different."

"Marco is a boy, you mean?"

"That's not what I mean, Gioia and you know it."

"Then what do you mean?"

A tense moment passed between the two of them. That had been exactly what he had meant, but he didn't want to admit it. He had spent years raising his daughter to believe that she could be anything that she wanted to be. How could he tell her now that there had been exceptions to the rule and that he had merely been hoping she wouldn't have noticed them? How could he say the only reason she couldn't achieve her dream had nothing to do with talent, but merely her chromosomal arrangement? "Gioia...a scout came to Marco. They got him a contract before he was even out of high school. If that hadn't happened, he might have gone to a different school, done something completely different..."

"But it did happen."

"Yes, and he's still taking classes. He's still majoring in business. He still has a backup plan. Things happen. You have to have a backup plan."

"I don't want..." Gioia began to protest, but her father cut her off.

"Everyone needs a backup plan."

She shook her head. He was sounding an awfully lot like her mother did and it was frustrating. Why was everyone telling her these things? "What about you? What was your backup plan?" Her voice had a certain venom to it. She was challenging him. She felt guilty immediately after doing it. Her father had tried very hard to finish college and achieve his dreams. Marco's birth had gotten in the way, but he still worked hard.

"You know what my backup plan was, Gioia," he said, keeping his voice far more steady than she expected. She knew what he was thinking and that it was hurting him to think it. "I'm living my backup plan."

"Don't you regret it?" she asked, venom gone, trying to sound genuinely interested.

"Regret you and Marco?" He shook his head, incredulously. "Not even for a minute."

"And what was your dream?" She had something of a vague idea. From the way he felt about baseball, she and Marco had figured that he had wanted to play too. It was obvious, but she wanted to hear it from him. He had never told her directly.

"Not all that different than yours." He looked uncomfortable with the question.

"Padre, please...what was your dream?"

Taking a deep breath, he stood up and began pacing around the kitchen. "When I was your age...I played baseball too. I..." He shook his head, laughing lightly again as a cover. "I wasn't like you and Marco though. I don't know where you get that from. Quite frankly, I was awful."

"I doubt that, Padre."

"No. Really. I was. I couldn't catch a thing."

"You threw with Marco and me when we were little. You had to..."

He raised a hand, cutting her off. "When I was in high school, I was the scorekeeper. Never got off the bench. I loved it though."

"But you still wanted to play?"

He shook his head. "No. I wanted to be in the big leagues, but not playing. I like the numbers and the statistics and the rules. I liked baseball and I liked a well played game. I wanted to be an umpire."

Gioia had to stifle a laugh. "You *wanted* to be an umpire?"

"Yes. I did..." He said sincerely.

"I didn't know people wanted to be umpires."

"How do you think they got to be them?"

"Accident," she suggested. "Punishment."

"Gioia..."

"It can't be enjoyable having people yelling at you all the time, calling you a bum, blaming you for every little thing that goes wrong."

He laughed genuinely this time. "No, but...they do that to the players too, Gioia. Pitchers especially catch a lot of shit."

She rolled her eyes, thinking back to a game last season where a ill timed walk had cost them the win. Several of the other girl's parents screamed at her and called her quite the barrage of names before Coach Yoder managed to get the team off the the field. She heard later that the only reason they didn't follow and continue hurling as many insults as possible is because they were all afraid of Marco. "Yeah...yeah...that happens."

"But yes. That was my dream. I wanted to be a umpire for Major League Baseball."

"And why didn't you?"

"It's not all that different than college. They want you to attend schools and pay for those schools...and there was Marco...and no time. I had to get a real job."

"You'd probably be making more money," Gioia mused. "They have to pay them well to put up with all of that, I bet."

"It wasn't expedient at the time. Grounds keeping didn't require anything extra and I could take IT classes at night down at the branch. "

"Why don't you do it now?" She asked carefully, genuinely curious. She and Marco were older now, it made sense to her that her father should pursue his dream now that he could.

He shrugged a bit, thinking that over. "It's crossed my mind from time to time, but...I'm too old."

"You're not *that* old."

"By the time I finished the required classes, I'd be 65 and I still don't have the money."

Gioia frowned. That tactic hadn't worked. "But don't you wish you could have done it?"

"That's not the point, Gioia."

"Don't you?"

He stopped walking a moment and sat down. He looked as though he were about to speak, but then he stood up again, throwing his hands out slightly frustrated, pacing toward the window. "Everyone, Gioia, every single person on this earth, at some point, wishes their lives had gone differently. The point is, did you live the best life you could with what you had? Did you at least try?" He stopped, turned back to the table. "But you still have to have a backup plan. Just in case."

She nodded. "Economics can be backup, but I still want to try to play baseball."

"How?" It felt to both of them like a cruel question, but it was a realistic one.

"I don't know, but I'll figure it out. I have more passion for the game than Marco. That has to count for something."

All her father would say before he left the room was "you should talk to your mother."

"What about her?" Gioia called after him, but he didn't answer. "Padre!" She called again. He still didn't answer. She wanted to scream. The whole exchange had frustrated her so much, she couldn't believe it. Her parents had always taught her that she could be anything that she wanted. Why where they were changing their minds on her now? It was ridiculous. She took the pamphlets and began looking them over again.

9

Despite everything, all the work that she had done, The East Central Ohio League championship came down to one single game: Tusky Valley vs. Strasburg, Gioia Rinaldi on the mound against Nora Boylan. It was already being called a pitcher's duel and the game hadn't even started. The field was tense and everyone could feel it. Every molecule in the air reverberated with it. Gioia swore that the energy could be felt by people who weren't actually at the game, maybe people who weren't even in the same county or state. She sat, waiting, in the locker room, staring intently at the ball in her glove. This was it. This was her last chance. Come spring it would be too late. She had to impress someone now. Immediately.

"Miss Rinaldi?" she heard Coach Yoder asking from behind her and Gioia snapped out of her reverie.

"Yes, Coach?"

"I'm hearing some rumors." She took a deep breath, clearly it was big news. "I'm hearing mutterings about there being someone from Ohio State here tonight."

Gioia couldn't believe her ears. "Ohio State?" She asked in a hushed whispered, as if saying such a thing out loud would make it untrue.

"That's what I'm hearing."

Her heart started to race a little. It was too much to be believed. "The Ohio State University? Not Ohio State Wizarding School or anything?"

Coach Yoder chuckled lightly. "The Buckeyes. Yes. One and the same."

"What are they doing here?"

"From what I can gather, they're here to see you."

"Me?" She couldn't believe it. She had been hoping for a school like Kent or Akron at the very best. This was different. This...was huge. "They're here to see me?"

"You, Gioia. Maybe that girl from Strasburg, but..." Coach Yoder trailed off. "Don't let her upstage you. You want that scout to want her and not you?"

She shook her head vigorously. "No. No, absolutely, not."

"That's what I wanted to hear."

"Where are they in the stands?"

"I'm not telling you. I don't want you playing up to them or even acting like you know. Play it up for everyone, okay? Win this game. This is a big opportunity for you."

'No need to tell me twice', Gioia thought, but she merely nodded in agreement. "For everyone," she added. "The whole team."

Coach Yoder nodded, an indulgent smile plastered to her face. "That's right. Now...come join the rest of the team."

"Can I have...just one more minute? I need to focus...my energy." It sounded silly to say, but Coach Yoder nodded.

"Take what you need, Gioia. Whatever time you need to win tonight."

She slipped out of the room and Gioia stood up. She felt a little weak kneed, but chalked it up to the news. It made her insides feel like bursting and more than anything she wanted to tell someone, but she couldn't. She knew she couldn't. Taking a deep breath, she started from the locker room.

"Good Luck," Cy whispered as she walked out the door.

She was shocked for just a second, but then looked over at him excitedly. "Ohio State is here!"

"Ohio State University, very nice. What did I tell you?"

"Thank you. Really. I mean it. Thank you."

"It wasn't me. I told you, if you showed up every Saturday morning, I'd see to it. You did all the work."

"You coached me."

"I wouldn't have bothered if you weren't talented. Now get out there and show Ohio State what you can do."

She reached out, shook his hand and grinning so proudly raced to join the other girls.

Nora Boylan had not pitched the last time the Tusky Valley Trojans had played the Strasburg Tigers. Something in the back of Gioia's mind was saying that this was on purpose. She had a very unique style that was hard for the Trojan batters to figure out. Jennifer sat back on the bench after striking out and shook her head. "It was like I couldn't tell what was up and what was down. She's a genius."

"Thanks," Gioia said, rolling her eyes.

"Oh don't get your pride up, the Tigers batters are going to be saying something similar about you, I'm sure. Not exactly doing wonders for my batting average that's all."

The next two outs were also strikeouts, easily. Everyone reporting the event was right. It was going to be a pitcher's duel after all. Or at least that was what Gioia hoped as she took the mound. She glanced over at the stands a moment wondering which of those people might be the one who held her future in his or her hands, but no one seemed to distinguish themselves.

She took a deep breath and looked away, promising herself that she wouldn't look back at the stands, at least not to find them, for the rest of the game. She had to keep her focus. Cy would tell her as much. Closing her eyes and breathing in again, she carefully shut out all of the sounds echoing from around the field. Suddenly, the cheers were gone, the heckles, everything went silent.

The first Strasburg batter stepped up to the plate. And so it began.

There was a silence over the whole crowd in the ninth inning. Gioia had hoped to have some sort of magic enough to make tonight a no hitter, but unfortunately, that wouldn't be the case. Her small comfort was that Nora Boylan wasn't going to show her up and get one either. She gave up a run to Jennifer in the fourth. The score was one to one.

As she took the mound, Gioia was confident that when it came Tusky Valley's turn to bat they would be able to get that last run in. Right now it was up to her to keep the score even and not allow anything to slip through. She knew that if she gave anything up, not only would she be letting her team down and forcing them to work harder, but the scout would see it. That would be what he or she remembered. She absolutely could not let that happen. It was far more pressure than she would ever admit she was feeling.

In a moment of weakness or perhaps fear, Gioia glanced out toward the stands, looking for some kind of familiar face. She wasn't trying to find the scout, but her family had to be there. Maybe if she caught a glimpse of her parents and Marco or even just Nellie, she would feel better. It was then that she saw it. Someone in the stands had a sign. How long they had been holding it up with no repercussions, she didn't know. She didn't want to know. It read "Gioia Rinaldi wears a strap on."

She winced. She couldn't help it. She knew there was a reason she told herself not to look. Still, how long had that been there? Everyone would have seen it. The scout might have seen it. Her parents might have seen it. It was far too horrifying a prospect. Shaking herself, she took a deep breath, trying to focus on the next three batters. Striking them out was all the mattered right now. It had to be.

One strike. Then another. They were easy fastballs, but she was scared to try a curve right now. She knew that her control wasn't what it should be with her thoughts running all over like they were, shaken as she was, but if she threw another fastball, the girl at the plate would definitely hit it. A curve it was, low and inside and it was called ball one.

She tried again. "Ball" she heard the umpire shout. Ball two.

Cy's voice was in the back of her mind. "Focus. Control is more important than anything else. Focus. Don't be so desperate."

"Don't be desperate," she whispered to herself. "Don't be desperate."

She prepared to throw and a voice came through the crowd though she had been trying so hard to block them out. "Hey, Rinaldi! Go ahead and walk her, can't wait to watch you make out later!"

She threw anyway. It was a hit. As the batter was called safe at first, her heart sank.

Shaking herself again, she turned back. It had only been a single. There were two more batters to go, but they could still get out of this. It wouldn't be all her fault. It couldn't be all her fault.

The next batter got a hit as well, but a very nicely done double play from short to second to first, made things a little easier on Gioia's mind. She looked toward

Coach Yoder in the dugout, who was watching her with a very concerned expression. It must have been pretty easy to see how shaken up she was. The look in Coach Yoder's eyes when Gioia's met them plainly read "Do you want me to pull you?"

Gioia shook her head and muttered, "No. Not yet." There was only one more to go. She had to try one last time.

The third batter came up to the plate and smirked out at Gioia. A minor panic ran through her. She closed her eyes trying to do as Cy had said and once again shut out everything else, to make the world around her go silent and to focus only on herself, the ball in her hand, and the catcher's mitt behind home plate. The lights flickered, but in her mind they went out. One strike. Then another. Desperately she tried not to hear a thing, not even the umpire's calls. She threw the final pitch. Strike three. Nothing could take the smile off her face.

10

For two weeks, they waited, hoping, almost knowingly for the offer from Ohio State to come. Everyone was practically certain it would happen, coming off an East Central Ohio League championship win like that. Even Mr. Peters, in spite of his better judgment, had stopped pushing Gioia to fill out more applications for a time. When the middle of November passed, however, without a word from anywhere, the time had come for Gioia to make a decision on her own about university. She knew it, but she still didn't feel like she was ready. There were other things, easily constructable distractions, to be concerned about for the moment. She had even allowed Nellie to drag her out to the store to get dresses for homecoming, though she had pretended to be protesting every minute, and claimed she had to work on college applications. Nellie knew better.

Nellie stepped out of the dressing room and spun around. The short navy blue tulle and taffeta skirt waved outward in a rather spectacular fashion. "What do you think?" She asked, very excited. Though she was seeking her friend's approval, she had already made her decision. This was going to be her homecoming dress.

Gioia clapped at the sight. "You look amazing."

"You sure?" She spun around again in the multiple mirrors for dramatic effect.

"Everyone will be falling at your feet."

"I seriously doubt that," Nellie said as she slipped back into the dressing room. "I'm getting it though." She returned to her everyday clothes, but still looked exceedingly proud to have that dress draped over her arm. "All right then, your turn."

Gioia shook her head. "No...I told you, I don't think I'm going."

"You have to go to homecoming. It's our senior year. It's a right of passage or something."

"I don't really care for dances."

Nellie sighed. "I don't have a date either. I'm not letting that stop me."

"It's not that," Gioia protested.

"Oh really? It's not?" Nellie raised a skeptical eyebrow. "What other reason could you possible have then?"

"I don't know. I just really don't want to go."

That response was unacceptable to Nellie. She paced over to the rack of dresses that had been recently returned. She pulled out several in Gioia's size and pushed them at her. "Go on..."

"No...Nellie..." Gioia passed them back.

"You don't go and you're giving them what they want." She pushed the dresses at her again. "Just what they expect of you, Gioia."

They both knew how bothersome such a thing would be to her. With a sigh, she took the dresses into the dressing room that Nellie had just vacated. None of these dress were ones that she would have chosen for herself. They were pretty, but they were all a bit too flashy or too revealing. "I don't know about this, Nellie."

"Just try them on! At least one of them, okay?"

After a several minutes of looking them over, Gioia ultimately decided on a yellow dress with a tied corset type top. The yellow would look good with her deep brown hair. "I'm only doing this to get you off my back!" She shouted as she slipped on the dress. Though when she saw her reflection, even she had to admit to herself that she looked good. Even the rhinestones, which she thought originally were a bit much, were a nice touch.

"Can I see it or what?" Nellie called.

With a deep breath, Gioia stepped out. "What do you think?"

"Spectacular," Nellie said in an awed voice.

"You're just saying that."

Nellie shook her head. "No. That's the one you're getting. Right there. You look like a princess."

"I haven't even decided I'm going yet."

"You have to. Everyone there will be kicking themselves with jealousy for not asking you and I want a chance to see that."

Gioia went over to the multiple mirrors and turned around examining the dress. Yes, it looked all right. Maybe not enough to shame the student body for leaving her dateless as Nellie claimed, but it looked all right. "All right. I guess I'll go, if only because it's senior year."

Nellie jumped up, excitedly. "Now let's get you some shoes."

Seeing there was no way out of the social experiment, Gioia nodded grudgingly. "I could use a new pair of shoes for softball too while we're at it."

Nellie rolled her eyes, but smiled anyway. "So long as you don't wear them with your dress."

"Of course not!" Gioia said, pretending to sound offended. "Cleats would scrape the gym floor."

Both girls laughed as they rushed off to look at what sort of shoes the store had to offer.

When the girls returned from their shopping trip, all the lights at the Rinaldi house were off. "Doesn't look like anyone's home," Gioia said, slightly confused. On a weekend night like this at least her mother was usually home. She always had some sort of big baking project for Sunday: six dozen cassata cupcakes or huge batches of marzipan, things like that.

"Want me to come in with you?" Nellie asked, turning off the engine of the car.

Gioia shook her head. "I'll be fine. I have a key."

"I'd feel better," Nellie said, climbing out of the car as well. "Something feels off."

"Don't tell me you're getting superstitious on me."

"You must be rubbing off." She waited as Gioia unlocked the door and the two girls pushed their way inside in the dark. "It's so eerie in here with no lights."

With a roll of her eyes, Gioia flicked on a switch. For a moment, she could have sworn she saw someone standing in the pantry. "Hello?" She asked immediately, her voice very concerned.

Nellie followed her gaze. "Someone's here?"

"I thought..." Whatever it was had disappeared, but a month of meeting with Cy Young's ghost for pitching practice had convinced her that anything was possible at this point. She started toward the pantry. "Who's there?"

"Should I call the police?"

Against her better judgment, Gioia shook her head. She didn't need it to be another ghost. "Maybe it was just a mouse."

Shaking her head, Nellie went for the phone. "I'm not being one of those stupid girls in horror movies that don't call the police."

Gioia waved a hand at her. "There's no one in here anyway..." Nellie didn't respond. She was holding the receiver in her hand and staring at the counter next to it with a deeply concerned expression. Gioia walked over. "If you say the line's dead."

Nellie merely pointed at the note stuck next to the phone. It was in her father's handwriting and it appeared to have been written so fast it was almost illegible, only four words, "Marco. Accident. Back Soon."

Gioia felt suddenly faint. "Marco?" No, if that ghost had been Marco...she didn't even want to imagine it. "No. Not Marco."

Nellie took her by the arm and started walking her to the table. "Come on, Gioia."

She didn't bother trying to resist. "He *has* to be okay. He has to be."

"I'm sure he is." Carefully, Nellie eased her friend into a chair. "Let me get you some water."

"Then why didn't he say in the note?"

"I'm sure your father was just in a hurry. I'm sure everything's just fine."

As if on cue, the phone rang. Gioia raced to it, knocking the chair over in the process. "Hello?" she asked, terrified.

"Gioia..." it was her mother on the other end of the line.

"Is he all right?" She asked immediately, clear panic in her voice.

"Gioia...calm down."

"Is he all right?" She demanded. "Is he alive?"

"Marco is alive," her mother said carefully. "He's very shaken. The doctors are doing some tests."

"What happened?"

"Your father is coming home to get you. He shouldn't be long."

"What happened?" She did not like the way that her question was being ignored. It made her all the more uneasy.

"Your father will bring you up."

"No...I have Nellie here. I'll be fine. You two should stay with Marco."

"He'll bring you up," she repeated. "Don't you want to see your brother?"

The thought of seeing her brother at a hospital terrified her to the core, but there was something in the way that her mother asked the question that scared her. Of course she wanted to see him. Had something happened that might limit that possibility? She thought again of the figure she thought she had seen. "He's going to be there awhile isn't he?"

"They are doing some tests," her mother said again. "Your father should be there to get you soon."

"All....All right," Gioia said carefully. There was no other way to respond.

"I have to go now."

"Of course, Madre."

"I love you, Gioia." Her voice was so sad.

"I love you too, Madre." The click came moments later. Gioia stood there still holding the receiver and trying not to cry.

"Is he all right?" Nellie asked very carefully after a few minutes.

Gioia nodded. "They're doing tests."

"Did she say what-" The deeply sad and frightened look on Gioia's face stopped her from finishing the question.

"No, Padre is coming to get me so I can go see him."

Nellie got up and went to her friend's side. Taking the receiver and hanging it up for her, she wrapped

Gioia into a tight hug. "He's okay. Everything's okay," she whispered over and over until Mr. Rinaldi arrived.

11

Neither Mr. Rinaldi nor Gioia said a word the entire drive to Akron General. Neither of them could bear to. When he had parked the car and turned off the engine, they both sat in silence for what felt like an eternity, neither of them willing to be the first to get out of the car. After it had grown far too long, Gioia looked over at her father. "What happened?"

He shook his head. "I'm not really sure. It was raining...he lost control of the car."

"Is he all right?"

"He's alive. That's what matters right now."

"Is he hurt?"

"Gioia...if you saw the car, you'd be saying the same thing. Please just...wait until we get inside."

She had never heard this sort of impatience in her father's voice before. It made her feel like something far worse was just around the corner and frightened her for her brother. "Of course, Padre. I'm sorry," she said in a voice barely loud enough to be heard as they finally climbed out of the car and started inside.

Gioia hated the smell of the hospital, the look of the hospital, the sound of the hospital, everything about the hospital. Ever since she had been a small girl, she had felt this way about hospitals. It seemed like every time she was in one something horrible happened. People were sick. People were dying. Nothing pleasant happened in a hospital. Still, she tried to keep this to herself as she followed her father to the waiting room where her mother was sitting.

Immediately, her mother ran over and gathered her close. "Gioia."

"Madre..."

Mr. Rinaldi put a hand on each of their shoulders. "Caterina...everything's going to be fine. Gioia is here. Marco is alive..."

Mrs. Rinaldi shook her head. "I know...I know..." Still, she held her daughter tightly to her as though she would never be willing to let go again.

"Did they say anything while I was gone?" Mr. Rinaldi asked.

Mrs. Rinaldi shook her head. "No...no...just that we have to wait."

"Can we see him yet?"

"Not yet."

"Is he awake?" Gioia interjected.

Both her parents exchanged nervous glances. "Not...yet..." her mother said in a very strained voice. "He..."

"He's unconscious...he hit his head," her father said, picking up for his wife. Tears were escaping her father's eyes. It was a sight Gioia hated to see.

"Padre..."

He shook his head, wiping his eyes as surreptitiously as possible. "Come sit down."

Gioia obliged. Her mother still not letting go of her, the three of them took seats together in the waiting room. She desperately wanted to ask for more information about what happened to her brother, but from the way her parents were acting, she didn't want to know.

She must have dozed off at some point because when she opened her eyes the room was much, much darker. She looked up at her parents. Both of them appeared to be asleep too. Otherwise the waiting room was deserted.

Then she realized it was not. Standing on the other side of the room was a man in a baseball uniform. It was clearly a Cleveland uniform, but it was vintage, definitely vintage. She had seen that particular design in the picture she had of the team from 1920 when they won their first World Series. It had always seemed an inspiring picture, but what someone in that uniform doing there now, she couldn't comprehend. Carefully, she slipped out of her mother's arms and started over. "Hello...?" she began.

He nodded slowly. "He's gonna be all right."

"You look familiar," she said immediately. "Who are you?"

He stepped back a bit, so that he might be further hidden by shadow. "No...you don't need to know. I'm here for Marco Rinaldi."

That wasn't the reaction she had been expecting. Cy hadn't been shy with her. He had appreciated her ability to see him. "I'm his sister. I'm Gioia," She said carefully, trying to sound reassuring. "Cy says that I can see you because..."

"You're meant to play." He nodded again. "I know. Tonight we're looking after your brother."

"We're?" Gioia looked around the room, trying to see if she could see any others, but there didn't appear to be anyone around.

"It's my turn to keep vigil. We take turns. There's an unfortunate amount of us."

"Baseball ghosts...or...?"

The already dim lights flickered a bit and he moved further into shadow. "Listen, Joy..."

"Gioia." She would put up with the mispronunciation from Cy Young, but not from someone she didn't know.

"Listen, Gioia," he repeated, slightly bitter about having to correct himself. "I'm glad that you can see me, but you have to let me keep my vigil. There's already too many of us mid career types, all right?"

She wasn't sure she liked that terminology. "What do you mean, mid career types?"

His tone as he proceeded was cautious, knowing exactly how she would react to what he was about to say. "I mean...those of us who died while we were still in our prime, still in the middle of our careers."

"Died?" Gioia asked, sounding panicked.

He knew that was what would happen. It was what always happened. "Marco Rinaldi is not going to die."

"Then what are you doing here?!" She demanded loudly. She was quiet surprised that no one heard her and woke up or came to see what the commotion was all about. Her father only responded with a snore.

"I told you, I'm keeping vigil."

"Why would you be keeping vigil if he wasn't going to die?"

"He's not. Now, if you would please..."

"How do you know? No one will even tell me how he is."

"He's not," the ghost repeated again carefully. "He might have a little playing trouble for a bit, but he's gonna come out of this. I should be jealous."

"Why? What happened to you?" She asked, genuinely curious.

"What sort of question is that to ask a person?"

Immediately, she felt guilty. It was a rather presumptuous question. "I'm just...trying to understand. Was it a car crash like Marco?"

"No," he answered plainly, looking into the room at the unconscious boy. It was almost as if it would be detrimental to take his eyes off of Marco, even for a second.

She didn't want to have to guess, but he didn't seem willing to give any further information. "Then-"

"It was a baseball," He said suddenly in the hopes that maybe if he was honest she would leave him alone.

"That can happen?" Somewhere in the back of her mind she seemed to remember this story. As it slowly came back to her, she opened her mouth to apologize, but he stopped her.

"Please," he said quietly. "I understand your worry, but your brother is going to be fine. Just go back to your seat and let me be here."

She still didn't quite understand what he was getting at, but she nodded and slowly turned back to her parents. If this man said her brother would be okay, she was willing to believe it. Slowly, eyes still on the baseball ghost, she curled back up with her mother. She knew better than to ask him any further. His presence meant her brother had even more eyes on him. That was what mattered at the moment.

Word came down the next morning that Marco was awake. The whole family was eager to get in to the room and check on him, but the nurse had to hold them back a little while. First the Rinaldi parents were able to visit, then Gioia would be allowed. She waited outside the room when her parents went inside, desperate to talk to her brother and of course yell at him for scaring her so much. She didn't feel very patient and peered in before she was told she could. Her father was clinging to his son's hand and her mother was standing behind him holding her husband's shoulders. Both of them were crying.

"Marco?" Gioia asked, not able to help herself.

He looked away from his parents, toward his sister standing in the doorway. "Hey there, Gioia..." he said weakly.

She had wanted to talk to him since she had seen the note, but now that he had acknowledged her, she felt oddly speechless. "What are you doing...crashing cars?" She forced out, trying to keep her tone as jovial as she possibly could, considering the circumstances.

"I wasn't even driving," he protested with a laugh. Her false tone had apparently worked. "Stop judging me."

"Is...he all right?" Gioia asked, slipping into the room, though the nurse hadn't yet given her the okay. She hated being left out of the family right now.

"You can direct that question to me, you know," Marco said, sounding a little put off.

Gioia shook her head and looked at him. "Are you all right?"

He shrugged slowly. "I hit my head. I guess they think that's a problem, but otherwise..."

"Broken arm..." Mr. Rinaldi added.

Gioia's eyes widened. "Not your arm!" she couldn't help exclaiming. Never mind that he had been unconscious for several hours. Her mind flew back to what the baseball ghost had told her: that he might have some difficulties playing baseball for awhile.

"Gioia," her mother said sternly. Her teeth were clenched in such a way that Gioia could clearly tell that she was putting on a brave front for Marco's benefit. "Your brother is alive. I think there are bigger things to be concerned with than his arm."

"But how will you play?"

"It will heal by spring," Marco said, not sounding nearly as concerned as she felt.

"Marco...baseball..."

"Gioia. It's not the end of the world. I'll be better by spring."

"Marco..." She wasn't sure why, but she could think of nothing else. Her mind kept going back to the ghost that she had seen earlier. Did that mean his career in baseball was going to end? She couldn't deal with it if that had been her.

Her mother stepped away and walked over to her. "If you boys will excuse us for a moment." She put her arm around Gioia's shoulders and steered her from the room. "Gioia..." she began when they had successfully made it out of earshot from the others.

"I'm sorry, Madre," she began, carefully examining the pattern gradients in the carpet. "...I don't know what I'm talking about."

"I should say not. Your brother could be dead right now and you're all up in arms about broken bones, excuse the expression."

"I don't want him to have to give up playing. He's barely started."

"Broken bones heal."

"But what if it doesn't heal right, or it takes too long and the team forgets him?" She knew her panic was misplaced, but she couldn't help herself. The disaster scenarios just wouldn't stop jumping into her brain.

"Gioia..."

"He's lucky. He gets to. It would kill me."

Mrs. Rinaldi pulled her daughter close and held her. "Gioia...this isn't the time."

"It isn't the time to be worried about Marco?"

"It's not Marco you're talking about, Gioia..." She shook her head. "We'll talk about this some other time. Right now we have to worry about your brother."

"Madre..." Gioia tried to pull away from her mother, but as she did so, she held on tighter. After a few moments, she simply gave in and began to cry. "I'm afraid to think about Marco."

Mrs Rinaldi nodded slowly, gently stroking her hair, trying to be comforting. "So am I, honey. So am I."

12

Cy was quiet at their next meeting. He didn't seem to know what to say and neither did Gioia. She had absolutely no focus, but he couldn't even bring himself to criticize it. He knew why she was this way right now as much as she did. After a long series of bad throws, she sat down on the mound and forcefully threw the ball into the outfield. "I can't do it today," she said bitterly. She felt as if she had absorbed her brother's broken arm.

Cy shook his head. "You have to push through this one, Gioia." It was the first time he had called her by her proper name.

"Gioia, huh?" She asked grimly.

"You...it's not a day for teasing."

"No, I suppose not." She stood up and though she didn't want to, she went out to retrieve the ball.

"It doesn't seem to be a day for pitching either." As much as it hurt him to say, they were getting nowhere. She was far too distracted.

"Don't say that," she said immediately, such urgency and venom in her voice.

"You have no concentration today. You're completely distracted." He frowned to himself. He hadn't wanted to criticize, but it was true. "And, it's understandable. It happens sometimes."

"Not to me. It can't."

"Your brother was just in a car crash."

"He's fine. He's home. He'll be back at school in a week. His arm will be better by spring. He'll still have everything he ever wanted." She surprised herself by how sour her tone was when saying those relatively good words.

Cy was a bit confused as well. "You sound bitter about that."

"He doesn't care. It doesn't even matter to him."

"I'm sure he's just glad to be alive. Most people are after a shock like that."

Gioia nodded slowly, sitting back down on the mound, trying to will time to go backward. "I hate that I feel like this."

He watched uncertain of what to say. It was all a little too emotional for him. "Gioia..."

"He could have died. My brother could have died and all I can think of is how I didn't get any offers from any college teams. I'm so selfish. I hate myself."

Still, he didn't know what to say. "Gioia...go on home to your family right now. They can help you more than I can."

"You promised," she replied bitterly. "You promised me that if I came here...if I worked with you every Saturday..."

He frowned. "It didn't work out like I expected, but there's still time."

"There's no time! It's over for me. I'm just gonna be some washed up ex-high school athlete who got the Trojans a championship one time and did nothing else."

"That's not true..."

"And it's going to be worse because I'm a girl and no one will even remember!"

"Gioia, please calm down."

"You promised me." She sounded positively venomous, enough to make Cy fearful despite the fact that he was already long dead.

"Maybe it will take more time than we thought."

She stood up and walked a few steps toward him then paced back to the mound. "Forget it. I'm going home. I'll figure something out." Cy didn't protest or try to stop her. He know that home was exactly where she needed to be right now.

She stormed into the kitchen and sat at the table again with the same pamphlets as before, pulling out the chair and throwing the folder down viciously. Unfortunately the rage in her movements didn't seemed to quell the disappointment or the sense of urgency she felt. She still had to make a decision. She still had to make it now. Nor did it take away her disappointment in herself for being so upset over this when her brother had just gotten out of the hospital a few days before. She felt narcissistic and she hated it all the more as the fear mounted. She hoped that if only she could make a decision about her future, these horrible feelings would go away.

"Gioia?" Her mother asked, walking in with a bag full of groceries from the farmers' market.

"Hello, Madre."

"You look a little down," she remarked carefully. Everyone in the house had been on pins and needles since the accident.

Gioia shook her head. "What's in the bag?"

Forcing a smile, Mrs. Rinaldi set the bag down on the table and began to take out a wide variety of several different types of squash. "Pumpkins for the typical fall orders, you know. Pies, muffins, all that nonsense, but for us, I was thinking butternut squash ravioli. I remember how much Marco liked it the last time. He could use a pick me up, I'm sure."

"Sounds fantastic...." Gioia continued to watch as her mother took almost ten squash out of the bag. "How much do you plan to make?"

Instead of answering, she examined the space on the table not covered in vegetables and picked up one of the pamphlets. "Cleveland State, huh?"

Gioia shrugged. "That's just one option. It's all gonna come down to financial aid."

Mrs. Rinaldi nodded, flipping through a few more of the pamphlets. "And still no word from Ohio State?"

"I don't want to talk about that."

"Gioia..."

"No, Madre, it was silly of Coach Yoder to even tell me. They could have been there for any reason. Probably Nora Boylan. She did really well that game. She threw...brilliantly. Even Jen couldn't hit her."

"I think you threw a great game as well," Mrs. Rinaldi said carefully, trying to reassure her daughter.

"They didn't seem to think so."

"Maybe if you give them a bit more time..."

Gioia shook her head. "Besides, Coach Yoder just said she heard rumors. They might not even have been there. Maybe she was mistaken."

Mrs. Rinaldi took her daughter's hand and squeezed it. "I don't want you to give up, Gioia. Not on your dream. Not yet."

"It's a silly dream. Everyone says so. Even Padre says so."

"He would never say any such thing. He knows better."

"He told me that I have to have a backup plan."

In a quiet voice, trying her best not to sound patronizing, Mrs. Rinaldi replied, "that's sensible and not the same thing as giving up."

There was something else about that conversation that jumped back into Gioia's mind. She hesitated, not sure if it would be appropriate, but ultimately decided to mention it, just in case it was important. "He also said that I should ask you about it."

"Me? Why me?"

"I don't know. That's just what he said."

Mrs. Rinaldi shook her head. "I didn't go to college, Gioia. I can't be of much help to you in making this sort of decision. I don't know why your father..."

"I asked him what his dream was," Gioia interrupted, hoping that would explain a little better.

"Ah..." an indulgent smile came over her face.

"What was yours?"

"I suppose you could guess." She gestured around the kitchen, but when Gioia continued to just watch her without commenting, she continued. "I wanted to be a chef and open my own restaurant."

"Your own restaurant?" That made perfect sense. Gioia didn't know why she had never thought of it. Her mother loved cooking; she had always known that. "You...got close."

Mrs. Rinaldi smiled, looking lost in thought, but then she shook her head. "I make pies and bread for the store. I'm very happy to do it."

"So, you got your dream?"

"It's not quite the same. You see..." She squeezed her daughter's hand once more. "They say cooking is women's work, but did you know that most gourmet chefs are men? I was afraid to try, Gioia. I was afraid to be told I couldn't do it. So I didn't." She took a deep breath and looked at Gioia very seriously. "I don't want you to be afraid just because you think they might doubt you. Don't give up yet."

Gioia shook her head, pulling her hand out of her mother's grasp. "Thousands of kids had my dream and had to face reality. I need to too."

"What am I going to do with you, Gioia?" She asked with a sigh.

Gioia wasn't really sure how to take in what her mother had said. She knew that she felt similarly about baseball to the way her mother felt about cooking. They both had the same passion for the thing they loved and the thing they loved could just as easily be a hobby as a career, but there was more to it than that. Her mother was saying she didn't try. Gioia, on the other hand, felt that she had tried and failed. That was different. Instead of addressing it, she merely shook her head again, trying to shake the thoughts away. "You can help me fill out these applications?" She suggested.

Her mother nodded a little. She didn't really know where to begin, but she did remember enough from helping Marco that there was a bit of hold over knowledge. "Which are we doing first?"

Gioia didn't want to admit that she wasn't sure. They all had good and bad qualities and it didn't make much of a difference to her now that playing ball was out of the question. She had been completely serious when she said that it would all come down to financial aid. With a sheepish shrug she said. "I'm not really sure."

Instead of scolding, Mrs. Rinaldi just smirked. "You need to think about that before we can do anything else."

"Which ones, Madre? Just tell me."

With great care and deliberation, Mrs. Rinaldi gathered up the pamphlets. "I say, you take these upstairs. Don't look at them down here with my dreams, look at them up there with yours. Let your pictures tell you what to do."

As much as her mother's insistent optimism annoyed her, Gioia nodded and took the college pamphlets up among her baseball shrine where the greats seemed only to mock her anymore and the die cut stars next to Progressive Field seemed merely a taunt. Her dreams were beyond her grasp.

Then suddenly, something struck her. She looked up at the pictures on the wall again, her eyes settling on the die cut stars. Her dreams might be beyond her grasp, but hers weren't the only dreams just out of reach. There was something she loved very desperately that struggled and struggled but couldn't seem to pull it off either. Instantly, a voice in her heart and a voice in her head made the same connection. She identified with her team. Her team didn't give up, even though it had been since before her father was born that they last wore championship rings. That didn't matter to her. What mattered was that every year, they tried again as though this time, at last, it could happen. That was part of why she'd loved them for so long. That was why should couldn't imagine following any other team.

She needed that inspiration and she needed to be close to them. Without hesitation, she picked up the application for Cleveland State University and began working.

PART TWO: AUDREY

13

Driving back to school was harder than ever this time. Audrey didn't want to leave her family right now, not even for a second. The doctors pretended that they were optimistic, but just hearing those three words had been enough to make her blood run cold. Amyotrophic lateral sclerosis. ALS. Of all the medical troubles that could have been the cause of her father's numb hand, this is the last one they would have expected and certainly on the top of the list of ones they didn't want to hear the doctor say.

"Poor circulation," all the doctors had been saying that for years. "Poor circulation." Over and over and over again. Every single time. And they would blame it on him too. "You have to exercise more." "Maybe a B12 deficiency." "You should eat more meat." As if a marathon runner was in need of more exercise. As if he could control what was to come. No one was sure of the cause of his ailments, but they certainly acted like they were, for years. Too many years. Some even told him that it was just because he was getting old. Thinking about it now made Audrey want to climb back through her memories and punch each of the doctors as hard as she could. Now it was too late. Not that catching it early would have helped, but maybe they could have tried. Maybe they could have done something. The only thing they could do now was, as the doctor said, "make him comfortable." She wanted to throw punches for those three words as well.

She was barely listening to the radio as 97.1 discussed recent trade acquisitions for the Tigers. That wasn't like her at all. Usually, she would gobble up this sort of thing, ready to hit the internet and find out as much as she could about the new players. She would report back to her father and they would have rowdy discussions over whether or not these choices would prove advantageous in the coming season. She was somewhat afraid to try that now. She didn't even know if he would even live to see the end of the season. The doctors had said it could be less than a year.

As she drove down Michigan Avenue, she suddenly found that she couldn't bear it any longer. Spurred on as if by some unknown force, Audrey pulled her car over and looked at the now empty lot that once contained her childhood. The place she used to come with her father when she was a young girl, when he would get $5 bleacher seats in center field. Those had been some of the best days that she could remember. Over the past few years, she had watched as it had been gradually torn down, slowly, piece by piece as if to draw out the torture. It was gone now. All that remained was an empty lot. It was a metaphor for everything in her life. The sheer crushing realization of this made her chest heavy. Tears began to well up in her eyes and she could do nothing to stop them. Everything that had once been good in her life was nothing more than an empty lot.

Before she really knew what she was doing, she opened the car door and started for a gap in the fence. She wandered through the overgrown grass and she could almost hear the echoes of times gone by. "This used to be home plate," she muttered to herself.

"I'm really impressed that you were able to find it so quickly," said a male voice. She wasn't quite sure where it was coming from. "There's not much left of the place is there?"

She froze, a sense of panic traveling the length of her spine. "I don't have any money," she muttered.

"I don't really need any money. Not really. Nobody really needs money where I am."

Carefully she turned toward the voice. The gathering night must have been playing tricks with her mind. The man standing there was almost translucent. "Who are you?"

He shrugged. "I could ask you the same question."

"I just..."

"I was supposed to meet someone here," he said quickly, cutting her off as he looked around uncertainly. There didn't appear to be anyone else around. It was like the whole area was deserted. "I was not expecting you."

Audrey was horrified. They only thing she could think was, *'I've walked into a drug deal.'* "I don't have any money," she repeated.

"I told you. I don't need money." He paused, looking her over with a smirk before continuing. "I'm...well...you see...I'm a ghost," he said, sounding actually a little amused by the fact. "What am I going to do with money?"

Audrey took a step back. She had not been expecting that at all. "A what?"

"A ghost," he repeated. "Should I say boo? Would that help?"

Again, Audrey shook her head in disbelief. "There's no such thing as ghosts."

"I beg to differ."

Taking a deep breath, Audrey began to look him over. He was dressed in a rather odd costume. It looked like a baseball uniform from the 1910s. She recognized the rather distinctive way they used to stylize the D from old photographs. In fact, a nagging sensation was telling her that she recognized *him* from the old photographs. Suddenly, his name came to her and she felt faint. "What are you doing here?"

He paced a bit around the area as if deciding how to answer her question. "Are you really going to make me explain? It's complicated and I'd really rather just get down to things."

Audrey watched as well. She didn't believe what he had said, but there was something odd about him. His body didn't actually seem present and his feet didn't seem to touch the ground in the right way. Everything about him was just slightly off from the physical world. An average person might not have noticed, but Audrey was a writer. She prided herself on being observant about that kind of thing. "What sort of things?" She asked skeptically.

He shrugged. "Baseball."

"You're kidding, right?" was all she could say. Audrey had never once in her life considered herself athletic. Not since the ill fated adventure that had been elementary school ballet.

He laughed somewhat cynically. "That's what I was thinking when I saw you."

Audrey grimaced. Sure, she knew she wasn't athletically built and she accepted that, but it was still hurtful to hear such things, even coming from a ghost. "Thanks," she replied sarcastically.

"No...no...sorry. That's not what I meant. You see, I was given a description and you don't exactly match it, but you're the only person here."

Audrey frowned a little. Sure, he said he was a ghost, but maybe she was dreaming. Maybe it was also some subconscious test concocted by her brain to see if she was still a nice person. "Who are you looking for?" she forced out.

He took out a slip of paper from his uniform pocket. "Tall, lanky boy. Glasses. Looks like he doesn't get outside much. Will be following his brother reluctantly and carrying a copy of Balzac. He will be the only one that can see you, but be careful because of the brother." He shrugged putting the paper away. "Balzac's my favorite. I really only took this assignment because of that. You don't, by chance, have a copy do you?"

She shook her head, smirking. "I didn't know baseball players commonly read Balzac. Most of the one's I've met probably haven't heard of him."

"That's a glowing commendation," he replied sarcastically.

She shrugged. "How come it said he'd be the only one who could see you?"

"It's complicated."

Audrey was not about to accept such an answer. "I'm clever. Try me."

He sighed and looked thoughtful a moment. "Well, you can only see us if you're supposed to be...involved with the game. We like to take care of our own. Baseball's a family...a dysfunctional family, but a family nonetheless. Maybe...secret society would be a better word."

"And I can see you because?"

"Apparently, you're one of our own."

"News to me," she said with a laugh.

He looked around once more and still not seeing the tall, lanky boy, he turned back to the girl of rather average height. "Why don't we play then?"

Audrey considered the proposition a moment and decided that this was all a strange sort of dream and it didn't matter anyway. "Sure. Why don't we?"

"You have any gear?" The ghost asked.

Audrey looked around. In a real dream bats, balls, gloves, and possibly a whole stadium full of screaming fans would appear to fulfill their needs. Nothing of the sort seemed to happen. "I wasn't really planning on coming here to play." She hadn't been planning to come there at all, actually.

"Then what use are you to me?" He said, half sarcastic, half frustrated, shaking his head.

"I'm...sorry?"

"I'm supposed to be helping someone get into baseball. If you're not going to play..."

For the first time all weekend, Audrey felt able to laugh and she did. "You're about twenty years too late, if you want to 'get me into' baseball, Mr. Crawford."

He looked quite taken aback by her sudden outburst of laughter. "Excuse me?"

"I love baseball. I've loved it my whole life."

"Oh?" He kicked at the dirt a little, eyes still watching her in confusion.

"Yeah, always have. It sorta calms me down, you know?"

The confused expression turned into one that appeared more intrigued. He'd never heard baseball described as a calming game. "I'm listening..."

Audrey wasn't sure she had the words to describe it properly. She could barely explain it to herself much less a stranger. Still, she didn't think she'd have many chances to talk about the game with Sam Crawford, so in spite of herself she pushed forward. "I feel...happy there."

"There?"

She shrugged. "Honestly, it's anywhere there's baseball really. There's just something about it, being near the game. No matter what bad thing happened that day. Maybe a boy broke your heart or you got bad grades. And it lasts too!" Once she had gotten started, she could stop. "Your whole life. When boys and grades don't matter anymore. Maybe you can't afford the new furnace so winter's gonna be cold or your life just won't start the way it's supposed to. Maybe you're lonely or bitter or everything is falling apart and you just found out someone you love is very sick. For a few hours, it's okay because there's baseball being played."

He smiled a little. "That sounds about right. You've got a way with words, ma'am."

She nodded slowly. "I should. I'm a writer."

"A writer?"

"Least I'm trying to be. Journalism's not exactly a booming career field right now."

"Journalist?" He seemed to start pacing "I never can be too sure about some journalists."

"Well, excuse me for living," she said with a laugh.

"It's nothing against you..."

Audrey crossed her arms defiantly. "It's not?"

He shook his head. "No. What you said was...different. A lot of them are always pouncing on us, saying that we're bunch of dirty losers, you know. Almost washed up."

"...a lot of you are."

"You know what I mean."

Audrey frowned. "Maybe I do. What does it matter?" They both stared at each other. Neither one wanting to speak next. It seemed like an age before Audrey finally broke the stand off. "It's getting late. I should probably get out of here."

Sam shrugged, looking thoughtful again. "Maybe...I'm not the one that was supposed to find you here. It had to have been someone else. Maybe you should come back."

"Maybe they should come find me." Taking a deep breath, she turned and walked to the car, trying desperately not to look back. Soon as she did, she was sure she would realize how deeply, deeply disturbed what had just happened was. She didn't want to think about what that potentially meant for her psyche.

14

When she got back to the dorm, Audrey was quite shaken. Between the news of the weekend and the incident at the old ballpark, she didn't know what to make of the world around her. She walked in, looking something akin to shell shocked and dropped her suitcase with a loud thud the instant the door closed. Her roommate, however, didn't acknowledge this. She didn't even look up from her seat on the couch where she was watching America's Next Top Model. There was also a strange smell in the room like day old cabbage mixed with orange soda. "Vanessa?" Audrey asked trying to sound as though nothing had happened. "Did you take the garbage out?"

"Huh?" Vanessa replied, still not looking up from the television.

"The garbage?" Audrey repeated, starting over in her direction in case she couldn't hear over the blaring of the television.

"What about it?"

Shouting seemed like a more effective method. "Did you take it out?!"

"Oh?" She still sounded confused, but muttered a response that sounded something like "Yeah, sure."

Audrey nodded slowly and walked into the kitchenette area to grab a soda. Contrary to Vanessa's statement, she saw a very clearly overflowing trashcan being swarmed with flies and groaned to herself, "Just lovely." The sink was also full of dirty dishes and additional flies. The half empty pizza box of indeterminate origin on the table seemed to be the only thing in the area that lacked them, in fact. "What did you do this weekend?" Audrey attempted to ask, hoping the response was something along the lines of "had to call the police because someone broke in a left a horrid mess."

Her question was only answered with a "shhhh"

With a roll of her eyes, Audrey began to unpack her suitcase at her desk, but the smell was nauseating. "Vanessa...seriously..."

"Can you wait until a commercial?" Vanessa's reply was so venomous, that if it wasn't for the fact that she hadn't moved an inch, Audrey would have sworn she was about to have her hands at her throat.

"This smell doesn't bother you at all?" No response followed. Audrey wanted to take a deep breath and count to ten, but she couldn't. She could barely breathe at all. She knew that she and Vanessa had very different ideas when it came to cleanliness, and she usually tried to wait it out. Vanessa would do the dishes when they ran out of bowls or something, but this was particularly bad. Against her better judgment, Audrey grabbed a bottle of body spray and generously sprayed it around the room before flopping down on her bed and pulling the blanket over her head. The weekend had been too much and she just wanted to sleep. She would deal with the mess in the morning. Knowing Vanessa, it would still be there.

The next morning Audrey woke to the ringing of her phone, followed immediately by a bitter shout from the other side of the room, exclaiming "turn your phone off! It's seven in the morning!"

Groggily, Audrey muttered something akin to an apology as she reached over and answered it. "Hello?"

"I'm sorry, did I wake you?" the voice on the other end asked, sounding extremely annoyed. Audrey didn't appreciate that. She felt she had far more right to be annoyed. Her first class wasn't until 10:30.

"Who is this?" she asked, still half asleep and unable to place the voice.

"It's the President, who do you think?"

"What...?" She asked incredulously. After yesterday though, anything seemed possible.

"It's your editor. Where is your story?" It clicked when he said it. Of course it was Tyler, who else would have the guts to bother anyone at seven on a Monday morning, but she didn't have a story. She had made sure to turn in everything for this issue last week.

"My...?"

Tyler didn't give her an opportunity to finish asking the question. His tone was incredibly confrontational. "I'm serious, Dawson. If you're not at this meeting, you better be covering something good. What's the good word on campus? What's going down?"

Audrey couldn't recall a meeting, but hated the thought of missing one. The paper was everything right now. "Tyler...I'm sorry. I had a rough weekend."

An exasperated sigh came from the other side of the receiver. "Just get your ass down here, Dawson. I don't really care about your weekend."

Though Vanessa was already awake, Audrey tried to be as ceremonially quiet as possible as she raced about getting dressed, gathering up her notebooks and laptop and running off across campus to the newspaper office.

The conference room of the paper office was already crammed full, but Audrey managed to shove her way toward the table without causing too significant a disruption. "I didn't know we had a meeting today," she hissed to Kate, one of her colleagues who covered mostly the opinion and political pages, as she snuck in.

"We didn't," Kate whispered back. "Ty called it. Emergency."

"Emergency?"

"Nice of you to finally join us, Dawson," Tyler said bitterly.

"When did you call this meeting?" She asked as she carefully situated herself at the table, trying to ignore his hostile tone.

"I sent out an e-mail yesterday morning."

Audrey nodded. "And for those of us who were not near a computer?" Spending the weekend in a hospital, going from doctor to doctor with her parents didn't actually leave much time for checking her e-mail.

"Have your e-mail forwarded to your smart phone, like I told you to."

"Because we all have smart phones. They're so cheap." She smirked at her own sarcasm. "Can you get off my back and get on with this?"

Tyler rolled his eyes."Fine. We need to make some changes." A low muttering went through the room. The last time Tyler tried to make changes was when he took over as editor and instituted a mandatory no adverbs policy. "Yesterday, our sports reporter, sent me this." He held up a print out that loudly proclaimed "The Red Wings Can Suck It".

"Now..." he continued. "I don't know how well everyone's eyesight is, but this article is laden with obscenities and contains no actual content. He then proceeded to tell me that if I changed a word, he would quit."

"Have we contacted a psychologist?" Kate suggested.

Tyler shrugged. "That's his problem. I'm not running this crap in my paper. It's not even hockey season."

"It's always hockey season around here," someone else added from the back of the room.

"I'm not running this. He quit, just like he promised. We need a new sports reporter."

"Can't we just cut sports? Does anyone read it?" someone suggested from the back of the room.

"Are you joking?" Tyler looked incredulous. Most everyone on the paper knew that sports was one of the more highly read sections, but really with some of the staff these days, he couldn't be too sure who was serious and who wasn't.

Several people laughed. "How about we just grab some A.P. Wire stories," said another.

Tyler knew very well that the head of the department would never stand for that. "This is supposed to be a learning experience. What do we learn from that?"

"Real newspapers do it all the time," yet another person piped in.

Tyler rolled his eyes. "So basically what I'm hearing right now is..."

"I'll do it," Audrey spoke up. Everyone in the room turned to look at her as though she had lost her mind. "Sports can dovetail pretty easily from entertainment, right?"

"It's a bit different," Tyler said carefully, suddenly feeling as though he was treading on dangerous ground. Something about the reporters lately made them seem a bit more unstable than usual.

"Seriously, what do I do now except review movies? It doesn't really keep me too busy. Sometimes they film them here and I actually have a story for a day, but honestly..."

"It's gonna have to be about more than how hot the football players are."

Audrey looked her him with a rather stunned and exasperated expression. "Did you really just say that to me?"

"You actually have to know something," Tyler went on. "You know, write about actual sports, the actual happenings of the actual game."

"And Carl's eight paragraphs on the declining quality of cheerleader's breasts was about actual sports?" Audrey challenged. The whole conference room had gone silent.

"Cheerleading is a sport."

"And their cup size has so much to do with their ability to do backflips..."

"Well, there's a reason Carl is no longer on the paper."

"-You- ran that story!"

Tyler nodded slowly. He didn't have a defense. "Does anyone else have any -actual- ideas for what we can do about the sports section."

No one said anything. Audrey crossed her arms and looked at him expectantly. "Looks like you don't have too many options, Tyler."

He sighed, knowing he had been backed into a corner. "We'll give you a try out. Get us a good first story and we'll see."

"All right," she crossed her arms and smirked at him, feeling rather pleased with herself. "Which game would you like me to cover?"

Tyler smirked back. "I can't send you to a game for a try-out. That's a waste of funds. Just make something up, something creative."

Audrey puzzled over that a moment, but nodded, accepting the challenge. "Might be a bit hard to top 'Red Wings Can Suck It', but I'll give it my best shot." Tyler grimaced at her words, but didn't say anything more on the matter.

15

This was the opportunity that Audrey had been waiting for a long time. The entertainment beat gave her the chance to watch a lot of movies and television, which might have been nice for some, but she got bored with it quickly. No one was interested in reading reviews of the ones she actually wanted to watch or what she really had to say about them anyway. It seemed as though no one wanted actual critiques either. All she had to do was drop one mention regarding the lack of representation of women of color on prime time television into a review of the fall line up, and her articles were suddenly getting special critiques for content for the next two months. She still wasn't sure why Tyler had such a problem with it, but he insisted that she keep everything jovial.

She hadn't been proud of a single piece she had written all year. That was, hopefully, about to change. She would be able to use these samples in her portfolio without feeling like she was severally underqualified. Not to mention the fact that she would finally be able to work with something she loved. She needed to get this right and she was willing to take a strange chance in order to do so, even if that chance seemed completely bizarre, so she stopped back at the old stadium again, this time with a purpose in mind, hoping that Sam would still be there.

"You know, it's funny," Audrey said as she leaned back against the fence, this time feeling a bit more confident. She didn't worry that people might react to the fact that she was talking to herself. It wasn't an entirely unheard of occurrence in this area. "My editor's name is Tyler. I can't stand him. He's so pretentious and thinks he's God's gift to his job. I heard you had a Ty you rather disliked as well..."

Almost from the instant she spoke the words, he was there, looking a bit on the perturbed side. Maybe his Balzac reader still hadn't come. "Dislike...may not be a strong enough world for how I felt about that man."

She smirked feeling quite proud of herself and took out a notebook. "Tell me more."

He shook his head, noticing that. "Oh no you don't. What are you trying to do here?"

"Just get your opinions on some things."

"My opinions?" He raised a skeptical eyebrow. "What sort of opinions?"

"How do you feel about the state of modern baseball? Any thoughts on the steroid issue?"

Sam scoffed at that. "Are you aware that I died in 1968?"

Audrey nodded with a shrug. "Yes. I knew that. Maybe not the exact date, but I knew that."

"And...you're going to interview me now because?"

When he put it that way, it sounded terribly silly, but when she had the idea originally, it had seemed a brilliant one: going down to the field, talking to the old players, getting their thoughts. "It'd make a really good novel," she suggested meekly, not ready to give up on the idea just yet.

"You're not writing a novel though, are you?"

She hated that he saw through that so easily. "Maybe someday," she said, slightly defensive, remembering how he mentioned a distaste for journalists. "But no, not at this particular instant."

"Then what are you looking for?"

"A story...for the paper."

"I knew it!"

"I need it to be really good. Tyler's he's...well, he's a bit of an ass and he doesn't think that a woman could be a good sports writer, which is rubbish, however, the matter still stands..." she trailed off realizing that Sam was biting back a laugh.

"Why don't you cover a game?" He suggested.

"What?"

"Isn't that what you're supposed to do?"

Audrey shook her head. "That's obvious. I need it to be really good. More than just a play-by-play. We can get those from the wire." She looked around at the empty lot again and felt her heart sink. Why did she keep coming here? It was just painful.

"And, you want me to help you?"

She frowned. Her idea seemed childish and adolescent now, like something she would have written in a high school class, not a grown up piece meant for her portfolio. "I don't really see how though. You're right. No one's going to believe that I actually talked to you. You're...dead. You're buried. I..."

"Let me work on it."

She smiled weakly. It was a kind offer, but she wasn't sure what a ghost would actually be able to accomplish on her behalf. "You don't have to."

"I'm not saying I'm going to get anything, so keep on your toes, but I don't know. Maybe I can push something in your direction?"

"You'd do that?"

He nodded sincerely. "I'm not such a bad guy. People may say I sent a congrats card to Nap Lajoie when he almost beat that...well, the point is I'm not a bad guy, and after what you said that night about baseball, well, there's a reason you can see us. I've gotta do something for you."

"You don't have to," she said again, tucking her notebook away. "I'm headed to work anyway. I should get going."

"That'll give me time to think about it."

She felt like an idiot, but nodded. "Thanks..." She started back to her car, but stopped for a moment. "You ever find your boy who reads Balzac?"

He shook his head. "Not yet, but I'm sure he'll show up eventually."

"Well, maybe I can help you with that later?"

"Write an article about it?"

"If you think it'll help. I'll make sure to tell him to come with his brother."

Sam shook his head. "That'll leave you without a ghost."

Audrey shrugged. "Maybe, but you weren't meant to be mine anyway, right?"

"Somebody is. You'll figure it out."

Audrey simply smiled and continued back to her car as he appeared to vanish yet again into the gathering dark.

16

The late shift at the coffee shop could be both the best and the worst: it depended on the crowd. Always less demanding than the morning crowds, it varied in make up. Some nights you got a group of students working late on their studies. They generally didn't bother the baristas much, expect for the occasional hope for refills. They also rarely tipped. Or there might be a bunch of kids making their way back home to the suburbs from a rock show in the city. They tended to get complicated drinks, if only to show off their supposed coffee knowledge to their friends. There were also the truckers or the clearly stoned night owls. Though on the surface they might not have seemed at all similar, both groups shared the predilection for ordering multiple bags full of ridiculous sugar laden pastries and large amounts of coffee. Whether it was for combating the munchies or keeping awake, it worked either way. There were many different kinds of people on any given night, and there were always different stories to tell. It was perfect for Audrey to practice gathering ideas for writing. It was horrible when it came to having morning classes or paper meetings.

It was midnight. She had been awake for almost sixteen hours and knew she had to be in visual communications class by 8:15 or face some serious consequences. She had already slept through it far too many times. To top it all off, she still had absolutely no ideas for her trial piece. It felt like she was making it harder than it was. She knew sports. She could talk about them all day long. It should be easy to crank out something, but she wanted the piece to be perfect. Perhaps that was why she wasn't expecting help when it arrived. She had just gotten done dealing with one of the regulars, who the baristas referred to a Mr. Mint Tea thanks to his tendency to gobble up gallons of it a night, when she noticed the register unattended. A young man was standing there looking rather confused and in a hurry. "Can I get you something to drink?" She asked as she rushed up to it, trying her best to make it clear this oversight wasn't her fault.

The man nodded. "That's all I need. The biggest cup of coffee you can find me."

"I think we can arrange that." She rang up a large regular coffee. "Here or to go?"

"To go if you would. I've got to get up early." He looked around surreptitiously. Audrey couldn't tell if he was looking for someone or was merely frazzled. "Flying out with the team for the game tomorrow."

Before Audrey could stop herself she exclaimed. "Shut up! That's not fair."

A tense moment of silence fell over them both as Audrey quickly calculated exactly how much tip she would not be getting. Then he began to laugh. "You're a fan, I take it?"

She nodded, looking sheepish. "Sorry, I-I've never been to an away game. I've always wanted to."

"You get tired of it after awhile."

"I can't ever imagine getting tired of it."

He laughed again at that. "Do you know who I am?"

As she began to really look at him, Audrey started to feel faint. The man who had just walked in and ordered from her coffee shop, where she worked, was a player for the Detroit Tigers. It was Armando Rhymes. "I..." She stopped herself when she realized that she had her pen held tightly in a death grip, but she had no idea how long she had been holding it that way. "You're..."

"So you do know me?" He smiled, clapping his hands together. "I was beginning to doubt myself."

She nodded quickly, her face turning multiple shades of red. "I...wasn't expecting to see you. Sometimes when you see people out of their...habitat..."

"I have a habitat?" He teased. "Like a real jungle cat?"

"You know what I mean..." She couldn't stop herself from continuing. "Can I have an autograph?"

He nodded. "Sure, but only if I can have my coffee first?"

"Deal!" She ran off into the back, mentally kicking herself for saying deal.

He smiled broadly at her when she brought the coffee out. "Thank you." He took out his wallet and nodded toward the cash register. "You gonna let me pay for it, right? Or are you going to call the *Free Press* and tell them I stole from you?"

"Oh, I'm sorry. I..." Audrey started back in that direction and then stopped, an idea coming to her. "Actually...."

"I was kidding about the paper." He looked a little nervous, she hoped it was just as a joke. She would never do such a thing. Not in that way.

"I know I mean, it can be on the house, I suppose." Her nerves were getting the best of her. "You are-"

He cut her off. "You can't give me free coffee for playing baseball. It's not that special. There's a homeless guy outside, give him coffee."

Something inside her stomach suddenly felt a bit guilty when he said that, as though her priorities were off, but she hadn't meant it that way at all. "We can give him coffee too, but..." What she really wanted was to ask him for an interview. It would be perfect for the paper: the impromptu thoughts of a professional ball player. She just couldn't make the words come out of her mouth. They kept getting trapped.

"I wouldn't have come in if it wasn't for him actually." He shook his head trailing off. "I almost thought he was wearing a vintage uniform for a second."

Audrey's mind lept. "A vintage uniform?"

"It's stupid. I wanted to ask him about it, but he ran off and then there was coffee."

Audrey forced herself to nod, mulling over the possibility that Armando Rhymes' sudden arrival might be Sam's doing. "Well, It'll be two dollars then. We'll send something out for him if he shows up."

He handed over the cash and smiled. "So, you know me, but...what's your name then?"

She blushed even harder. "Audrey. Audrey Dawson."

"You come to the games, Audrey Dawson?"

"When I can..."

"What about Sunday's game?" He held up a piece of paper, pretending it was a ticket.

For a moment she entertained the idea, but then she shook her head. "I can't accept that."

"No strings, I promise."

"I already have a ticket for Sunday," she lied.

"I can come up with another day."

The fact that he seemed so eager, completely out of the blue to do some sort of favor for her was a little disconcerting. Sure he had said no strings, but did he really mean it? "Why?"

"You just seemed like you could use something nice happening to you. That's all."

"But why?" She pushed.

"I don't know. Maybe I'm just in that kind of mood, I guess. I'm not typically the type of guy who goes and talks to random drunks in old uniforms..."

Audrey didn't want to say anything about how that little fact wasn't actually surprising, but it wasn't, so she nodded as if to say *I figured.* "You're feeling charitable?" She suggested.

"That's right," He agreed. "Charitable."

"That's kind of you...but I don't really need you to be charitable. I need to finish my shift and not fall asleep in class tomorrow."

With a slight laugh, he nodded. "I can accept that. I need to catch a plane anyway, but I will think of something else. You can hold me to that."

Suddenly her brain felt like someone had poured hot coffee over it. The stalling had almost certainly been to give her time to ask about the paper. She tried desperately to gather her courage, to say something about needing an interview, but she felt her vocal chords unable to vibrate. She nodded and mentally kicked herself again as he left. Maybe the fact that he came in at all would be a decent enough story. Tyler wouldn't be particularly impressed, but at least it would be an angle.

17

"I'm home!" Audrey called out when she opened the door to her parents house. Instead of the typical smells of her home such as her mother's favorite cinnamon apple candles, she was only greeted by an oddly institutional smell, reminiscent of hospital rooms and nursing homes. This was not a welcoming scent at all. "I'm home..." she repeated much more quietly.

Her mother peered out from around the corner, her face plastered over with a fake smile. "Audrey, doll, don't you have class?"

She shook her head, setting her book bag down. "Monday, Wednesday and Thursday are class. Weekends are for writing, working...and helping you here."

"Oh no you don't." Mrs. Dawson shook her head immediately, disapproving of this development.

"Mother..."

"I mean it. Your jobs are to work and study. I don't want you getting behind because of all this."

Audrey locked eyes with her mother. They were both stubborn women. It was bound to be quite the stand off in the future. She decided to change the subject for now. "Why does it smell like a hospital in here?"

Her mother sighed. "Don't let him hear you talking like that."

"It's Dad?"

"We decided it might be better if we got him a hospital bed...and set it up down here. That way there's easy access to the kitchen and no stairs..."

"No stairs?" Audrey's heart sank. She remembered her father running the Detroit marathon and now he couldn't walk up stairs? She simply couldn't fathom it.

"Oh, he says he's fine with them, but I'd rather have it handled before he hurts himself."

Audrey shook her head. She didn't like the sound of that idea at all. The very thought of her father's disease getting to the point that he couldn't climb stairs terrified her. "Mama..."

"Is that my Audrey I hear?" her father's voice called from the living room.

Audrey looked up at her mother, who nodded her okay, and then she started in to see him. He was lying in the bed already, propped up to watch television though it didn't seem like he was paying any sort of attention to the images flashing across the screen. He looked far more frail than she liked to think of him. She wanted to remember the strong man who had always stood by her side. This was hard. "I'm here, Daddy."

He grinned at her. "This bed has a remote control. I could probably get used to this if they continue to force me."

She shook her head. There was no way her father was going to 'get used to this.' "I get the feeling you're going to be fighting them every step of the way, aren't you?"

"You've got to, my girl. You can't just accept what life gives you." He sat up some more and gestured toward a seat nearby.

Audrey took it without question. "Speaking of which..."

"Yes?" He looked intrigued, hopeful even. A bit of good news was just what he needed.

"I'm going out for a new spot on the paper. I'm trying to be their new sports reporter."

The laugh that followed wasn't cruel, merely surprised. "Sports reporter? My Audrey? My 'the high school football team is destroying the fabric of everything I hold dear' Audrey?"

"They were taking all the arts funding, but I had nothing against football in general," she said, attempting to explain. "And, I don't know, but I think I'd be good."

"I haven't the slightest doubt. I'm just a bit surprised; that's all. What did they say when they gave you the job?"

"It's just a trial piece. I don't have the job yet."

"Yet. What did they say?"

Audrey shook her head. Her father's unceasing optimism about her future tended toward irritating, but at the moment it was a welcome distraction. "Oh, they gave me some line about being a girl..."

"Of course they did."

"And, you know, about needing to write about things other than how hot the players are..."

"Oh don't give me that. I read that slop that young man wrote about the cheerleaders." He shook his head disdainfully. "Probably thought he was quite the man for writing it, but he came off as nothing more than a child."

"That's the opening we're filling, actually."

"Congratulations. Someone finally had sense to give someone with actual talent the job."

"I don't have the job yet, Daddy."

"Yet." He said in a definitive way. There was to be no arguing with him on that note.

Audrey just smiled and shook her head. She knew better than to even try. "How are you feeling?"

"I'm feeling fantastic. Never better."

"Mother said you were being stubborn about the stairs."

"I don't see..." He began to explain, but Audrey cut him off quickly.

"You know what the doctors said. You're not supposed to strain yourself too much. If something is troublesome, you're supposed to let us help you."

"Stairs are not troublesome. Your mother worries too much." He shook his head and reached for the glass of water on the nightstand. Audrey jumped up and handed it to him instead. "And you do too."

She frowned, most definitely not agreeing. She didn't think she was doing enough. "I'm just going to be here for you, okay?"

"This better not be getting in the way of your studies."

"You let me worry about that, all right?" She took the glass, set it back down again and grabbed the television remote. She hoped that distracting him would help. "How about we watch some baseball? Just like old times."

Her father smiled and took his daughter's hand. "This'll be the year, Audrey. This'll be the year the Tiger's make it again. I can feel it in my bones."

"You say that every year."

"But this year...the bones have been particularly communicative."

Audrey forced a laugh, knowing he was trying to make light of his illness. "I don't think it's your bones."

"It's my bones, if I say it's my bones. And, it's the year, if I say it's the year." He attempted to squeeze her hand and though she could barely feel it, she knew what he meant. She squeezed back. Maybe he was right this time. It was only fair.

Her father had drifted off to sleep before the game had ended and while he had been the snoring type most of his life, his labored breathing terrified Audrey now that she had something else to link it to. With a deep frown, she kissed her father's forehead and slipped out.

Back in her own room she had a radio stored away where she could finish listening to the happenings of the game on her own. It was a pretty old one, having served as her vehicle to baseball since childhood, back when her mother would send her to bed before the games were over, but it was well loved.

She laid back on her bed, arms behind her head, listening to the words wash over her, trying to will time to go backwards. She'd often done this before. It never seemed to work in the way that she wanted. Time only seemed to progress onward, taking all from her that it could take. As she mulled that over, something suddenly struck her about this moment she was having. Here she was, caught somewhere between child and adult, wanting to move forward and at the same time wanting to slip backwards to simpler times. There was only one bridge between the chapters of her life.

With a deep breath she sat up and took out her notebook and pen. She began to scribble. The words came slowly at first, almost as if she were hesitating, afraid to put down how she really felt. Then without warning, they began to pour out of her. She wrote about the hardworking team she'd followed all her life and how much they reminded her of the hardworking city in which she grew up. Baseball was a metaphor for her city, her life, the heartbreak of every single teeter-tottering day between stability and fear.

If this wasn't the perfect trial article that Tyler was looking for, it was his loss. She had never been more proud of a single piece of her other writings.

18

Instead of e-mailing Tyler the piece, Audrey proudly walked into the paper office before her first class and placed the completed article on his desk with a grin. It felt so much more professional. Not to mention that this way she got to see the look on his face when she read it and he couldn't ignore her standing right in front of him like he could an e-mail.

"What's this?" He asked, not looking away from the laptop screen in front of him. The tiny speakers were relaying noises that sounded an awful lot like the explosions and made up battle language in some fantasy game, so she was sure he wasn't doing anything related to the paper

"It's my trial article," she said proudly.

"Already?"

She shook her head. "I was actually worried that you were going to think it was late. We have an issue to put out, don't we?" Still, he did not look up, so Audrey dropped the paper onto his computer, in front of the screen.

Somewhat annoyed, he nodded, picking up the paper and looking it over, skimming as quickly as he could. "Mmmmhm," he said several times, nodding and shrugging so much that Audrey felt she was about to burst. "Yep...sure...all right."

"Gonna comment on every line?"

He narrowed his eyes at her and shrugged. "You could have e-mailed it if you were in a hurry." And back to reading he went, still saying "mmmmhm" every few seconds. Finally, he set the paper down. "We'll it's not exactly specific."

"What do you mean?"

"Well, you'd have to write about...I don't know...a game that actually occurred."

Audrey was taken aback by this. This request was the exact opposite of what he had initially asked for. "You told me to do something creative. That it would be a waste of funds..."

"You could have watched something on TV," he said with a shrug.

"You told me to be creative," she repeated.

Tyler shook his head. "Look, it's a good essay..."

"But it's not 500 words about cheerleaders is what you're saying?"

"That's not what I'm saying."

"What do you want me to do? You want me to write a play-by-play? I can write a play-by-play. I can write a damn good play-by-play."

"There's not exactly time..."

"I could write it tonight. I could write it right now if you want." She pointed dramatically to the row of staff computers by the window. "I could sit down at the desk over there, and pound it out. I remember every second of last night's game."

"Dawson..." he said gently.

She started over to the desk and turned on the computer. She ignored his protests and pretended that she was very interested in the boot up noise. "Let's see, where should I begin. Should I perhaps start off with the lax pitching in the first? I know it improved significantly, but that first inning almost blew the game..."

"Dawson!" he shouted this time so loudly that she could have sworn the windows shook.

"Yes, Tyler?" she asked, finally looking back at him.

"I decided I'm going to take sports myself."

"What?" That didn't make any sense to her at all. "You're the editor of the whole paper, why do you need sports?"

"I like going to the games..."

"You're seriously going to sacrifice quality for perks? It's a job, Tyler."

He shook his head. "I don't think I'll be sacrificing quality. I'll still be able to do our sports features. Nobody is looking to us for serious play-by-plays. They can get that on the internet."

"Some people do." She couldn't believe what she was hearing. He didn't want play-by-plays, but he didn't want her piece either? Did he intend to give her a chance at all?

"And those people aren't going to accept having their play-by-plays written by a girl. I have to do what's best for the paper," he said it all so casually, like it was merely the facts of life. "We'll work it out. Stick to Arts and Entertainment. It's what you're good at."

Feeling a strange rage bubbling up inside her, Audrey stormed over to his desk and grabbed her article. "If you're not going to run it, you can't have it."

He didn't seem fazed by the incident. "Sure...put it in your portfolio. It's a good feature sample. It's just not what I'm looking for."

"Nothing would have been," she muttered as she marched out. The feeling was slowly turning from rage to determination. She needed a plan. She had never planned to be a sportswriter, but now she wasn't going to let anyone stand in her way.

She stormed back into her room and threw down her book bag. The whole way back to the dorm, an idea had been spinning through her brain and she simply couldn't stop it. As she walked, it grew more and more developed. She began to see page layouts. She began to see photographs. In her head it was all coming together. If she wasn't able to write the pieces she wanted for the paper, she would write them for herself, for her own paper in a way. New media was taking over and changing everything. It would make sense to go out into the world of journalism with blogging experience.

Sitting down at the computer, she got immediately to work. She didn't notice the time ticking by when she missed lunch or her two o'clock class or dinner. She didn't notice Vanessa coming back with several of her friends, making a popcorn and soda mess all over the common living area. She didn't even notice when they asked her if she wanted to go with them to a party. "Suit yourself," Vanessa said as she grabbed her purse and left. Audrey never once looked up.

"You're still on the computer?" Vanessa asked when she reappeared several hours later around one in the morning. "What the hell are you working on?"

Audrey was putting the finishing touches on the page and glanced at the clock. She couldn't believe it. "Just a project."

"Not like you to leave things 'til the last minute."

"Oh it's not last minute. I technically have plenty of time." Regardless, it felt terribly urgent.

"Then why are you working on it now?" Vanessa asked in an incredulous voice as she peeled off the high heeled boots she had been wearing.

Audrey shook her head. She wasn't sure how to explain the fever that had overtaken her earlier in the day. She had to finish creating it now or it would haunt her until she did. "Well, I've decided to start a blog."

Vanessa nodded, looking impressed. "Nice. Going to become the next internet sensation?"

"Not...that kind of blog."

Vanessa shrugged. She must have supposed it was still interesting because she walked up and peered at the computer over her roommate's shoulder. "A sports blog?!"

Audrey nodded. "Specifically baseball, but I could touch on other things too, if I want."

"Don't guys have sports blogs?"

"Apparently women do too, because I'm a woman and I now have one." Audrey smirked proudly, finally stepping away from the glowing screen and keyboard for the first time in hours. "Isn't the internet wonderful?"

Popcorn went flying as Vanessa plopped down on the sofa. "You really think anyone's going to read it?"

Audrey began picking up her things and started toward her bed. "Probably not, but I'm gonna write it anyway. I like writing about baseball."

"If you write it they will come, huh?" Vanessa muttered, picking up a magazine from the floor to read.

Audrey had to admit that she was a little surprised that Vanessa knew the line well enough to put it in context, but it suited."Precisely," she said and closed her eyes. "Precisely."

19

How she got into the park so early, Audrey didn't know and Audrey didn't care. She had never been able to see the Tigers batting practice before and it was exhilarating. She bypassed all of the various amusements and hurried as close as she would be allowed. Much to her surprise, she found herself tremendously close to the outfield. There was a throng of other onlookers as well, all hoping to maybe snag an autograph if they got someone's attention. Audrey leaned against the railing, eyes wide, ecstatic to be this close to the field. She knew that she would have to go up to her seat on the third level soon enough, but for now she was inches from the action. With care she took out her notebook and began to scribble a few minor details about the game ahead: the line up, the wind speed, the current location of the sun and such things.

It might be typical day-to-day game reporting, but she was going to make it shine.

"Dawson!" she heard someone calling as she wrote. She almost looked up, but it sounded like it was coming from the field. They had to mean someone else. Dawson wasn't exactly an uncommon last name, after all. "Audrey Dawson!"

That was distinct enough, however. She looked up from her notebook and out toward the field where the voice was coming from. She didn't see anyone she knew, of course, and shook her head. "If this is another ghost," she muttered to herself.

"Audrey Dawson! Pay attention!" Suddenly a baseball was flying in her direction. Instinctively, she caught it, but sheer terror showed on her face. She did not like the idea of a baseball moving toward her head.

"What was that?!" She screamed, utterly horrified. For a second she was sure that she had seen her life flash before her eyes.

Then she heard laughter and clearly saw Armando Rhymes, the baseball player who had come into her coffee shop the other night. "I think it was a baseball, Audrey Dawson," he teased, walking toward where she was standing.

"Right," she muttered, tossing the ball vaguely back in his direction.

"That was a damn good catch." The throw was not. It landed several feet away from him. He just smiled though and leisurely went over to fetch it.

"Blame the adrenaline. It was catch it or die." Her stomach was doing a rather extravagant series of flip flops, cartwheels and various other acrobatics. She couldn't believe she was talking to an actual member of the team she had been following her entire life.

"Catch it or die..." he mused. "That's how it always is out here."

She raised a skeptical eyebrow. "Always? I've seen missed catches plenty of times. Some of them looked pretty easy."

"Well, for starters," he said with a slight smirk. "Some people are about as good at throwing the ball as you are."

Audrey leveled a glare at him. "Glad to know I'm major league caliber." She picked her notebook back up from where it had tumbled as she caught the ball. "Now, tell me what you mean by catch it or die?"

He raised an eyebrow. "Hold up, you're press? I thought you were a barista?"

"I am a barista."

"Then what's with the notebook?"

"I'm also a communications major on the Wayne State paper." It wasn't exactly a lie. That wasn't why she was there today, but she wasn't sure how he would react to her saying she was a blogger.

"So you're press?"

"Something like that..."

"Something like that," he repeated, looking at her skeptically as he said the words, as slight disbelief in his tone. Audrey found it rather irritating and all she could think of was Tyler saying that people wouldn't accept a woman in her role.

"If you don't want to talk to me..."

He glanced back at his teammates, several of them seemed to be watching him uncertainly. "I have to get back, but since you're all right, here's your quote. In baseball, you've got to work hard and perform everyday. Yesterday doesn't matter. Today is today."

"Carpe Diem," she said, scribbling that down and a few notes to herself. "Thank you."

"Carpe Diem, Audrey Dawson," was all he said before rushing away to rejoin the others.

Several of her fellow autograph seekers were staring at her with confused looks of jealousy plastered to their faces in such a way that they could have gotten them all into a wax museum. She smirked back at them, wanting to say something incredibly clever, but completely unable to find the right words. Instead, she hurried out of the crowd and started for her seats in the upper deck.

20

"Attention: Seeking sports fans who also enjoy Balzac" ran as her headline that day. She was so proud. The article might have seemed weird and vague, but she felt it was only fair to Sam to use her new found power to try. Somewhere out there was a new slugger poised to take on the baseball world, if Sam could find him, and after all he had done for her...

"One of the greatest sluggers of the dead-ball era, Sam Crawford once said in an interview that he enjoyed reading Balzac..." she wrote, smirking to herself at the style she was trying desperately to convey.

"You have got to be kidding me," her mother said peering over her shoulder at the words she had written so far. "That's what all this hype is about?"

Audrey looked up and her, slightly confused. "Hype?"

"Your father's doctor, Dr. Cochrane, said he had been reading your blog lately. He says you're brilliant."

This revelation fell over Audrey like she had been doused with a bucket of ice water. She'd only met her father's most recent doctor in passing on the day he had been given his diagnosis and she hadn't seen him since. "Who's reading my blog?"

"Your father's doctor. He was raving about some piece you wrote about the here today gone tomorrow attitude toward achievement that some ballplayer has or something."

"Armando Rhymes. Yeah." She smiled to herself. That one had been particularly good. 800 words about Rhymes' attitude and how so often it was only that one instant on the field that everyone remembered a player for until career's end. She had personally thought it profound and she was glad that someone was reading.

"You smiled when you said his name..." Her mother jumped in suddenly. Her voice had an odd little matchmaker tone to it, like when she had tried to fix her up with their neighbor's son for prom. Audrey hated that tone.

She rolled her eyes. "Mother. He's a baseball player."

"That doesn't mean anything."

"Just don't let dad hear you talking like that."

Her mother sat down on the bed and watched Audrey post the piece. Audrey knew she wanted to say more, but didn't want to engage in the discussion at the moment. The silence in the room was tense. She was incredibly grateful when she heard the phone ringing and let out a sigh of relief after her mother left to go answer it.

"Audrey?!" Her mother called after only a moment's reprieve.

With another roll of her eyes, she got up from her desk and started into the room. "Mom, I really don't want to talk about my future matrimonial prospects right now," she said exasperatedly as she entered. It was then that she realized her mother was still holding the phone, a hand over the speaker. "For me?"

"Apparently the privacy minded people in your newspaper office thought it would be okay to give this gentleman your number. I can't imagine why they would do that..."

"Who is it?" She asked, rather confused by the whole thing. People rarely called her at home anymore. The only reason the paper had this number was for emergency contact purposes.

"It's a Mr. Fleming. He says that he's a public relations director for a certain...baseball club we all know and love?"

A weird feeling of panic suddenly overcame her. Was this man about to berate her for writing about the Tigers unofficially? That was impossible, wasn't it? There was no way anyone in the actual Tigers organization was reading her blog or even knew about it. There was absolutely no way. "I..." but before she could protest any further, her mother had pushed the phone into her hands. "H-hello," she stammered.

"This is Miss Dawson?"

"This is she." She could feel the floor slipping out from under her. Her legs suddenly felt like they could no longer support the weight of her body.

"Miss Dawson, glad I finally got a hold of you. I just wanted to say that I and a number of others in the office, in fact, have taken recently to reading your blog."

"My blog?"

"You are the author of *This Urban Jungle* are you not?"

"Yes...I...I am."

"The article you put up the other day on Ramos' fielding style was inspired. "

"...Thank you." She really wasn't sure how to take all this. There had to be a reason he was calling, but now that he wasn't yelling at her or threatening to sue, she could not comprehend what that might be.

"What's your readership like?"

"Well..." She hadn't checked her hit count recently. Constantly checking her traffic made her feel narcissistic and tired. After hitting refresh every few minutes during those first weeks, she had grown tired with watching the slow small numbers, so she stopped checking. "I imagine my audience is baseball fans." she said as a stall tactic.

He laughed. "No, I don't believe it. All this time I thought I was reading a fashion blog."

Usually she was good with sarcasm. As a barista, she had to be, but the whole incident had caught her completely off guard and she wasn't on her game. "I haven't...crunched the numbers recently, sir." Mentally, she kicked herself for saying sir. It slipped in her anxiousness.

"You really don't need to call me sir. That makes me very uncomfortable."

"I'm sorry..."

"Don't be sorry. Just letting you know." He laughed again. "I'm just calling because I like what I see and I could use an intern on the new media front."

Audrey felt herself becoming faint again. This time for an entirely different reason. "An intern?" She saw her mother look up with a rather pleased expression.

"Someone's gotta handle this social media thing and if you've already got a following..."

A blush began to rise in her cheeks. "I don't know if I have a following exactly."

"Are you interested?"

"I..."

"You don't have to give the answer right away, but let me know soon. I can get you set up in time for the next home stand, hopefully."

Deep down, she knew she should wait. She knew that she should try to make herself appear important and not too eager, say she had to check her schedule that sort of thing, but she simply couldn't help exclaiming. "Absolutely! I'm definitely interested."

"Great!" He seemed genuinely pleased by her enthusiasm. "That's wonderful. We can meet to go over the details when you get to the park, but otherwise...you can start on Monday."

"Monday..." Her head was spinning and she suddenly got the sensation that she was flying. For all of the emotions of this one phone call, it was a wonder she hadn't gotten sick. She looked over at her mother, whose eyes were wide, both with excitement and expectation. "Monday. Absolutely. I'll be there."

"Administration door. I'll leave your name at the desk , but in case, ask for Tim Fleming."

"Got it. Monday. Administration door."

"That's on the Montcalm side, if you don't know."

She didn't, but had been too embarrassed to ask. "Thanks."

"I'll see you then."

Audrey nodded, but quickly remembered that a nod could not be heard through the phone and instead said. "I'm looking forward to it. Thank you for the opportunity."

After hanging up the phone, she looked at her mother. "I really think I have to lie down."

Her mother nodded with quite the smile. "Can I tell your father?"

"Let me...just...in a minute?" She rushed back into her room. It was going to take a little while for her to process what had just happened.

Audrey hadn't been able to fully explain to her father why she didn't get the sports reporting job at the newspaper originally. He had been enraged by the news and it was a rare thing for Audrey to see her father truly angry. She decided to approach this very carefully.

Expecting him to be asleep or at least resting, she slipped into the room and was surprised to see that he was up and reading. "What's interesting?" she asked, interrupting his solitude.

"Book about the 1968 team." He marked the page and held up the book so she can could see the cover.

"Learning anything?"

"Keep learning until you die, Audrey, doll. Though that's closer for some of us than others."

"Don't talk like that," Audrey said immediately. "Don't you dare talk like that."

Her father shook his head and reached for his daughter's hand. "Audrey, please, don't be upset."

"Daddy, I...how can you expect me not to be upset?" She took a deep breath. This hadn't been the plan at all. "This wasn't want I wanted to talk about anyway."

"You need a reason to talk to your dad?"

"You know what I mean..."

He nodded. "Just teasing. Go on, Audrey."

"I just got a call offering me a new job," she said carefully, just as she had planned.

Luckily, he proceeded by asking exactly what he had in Audrey's preplanned conversation."A new job?"

"Yes. It's because of the writing I've been doing for the blog."

"Because that horrid boy won't let a talented woman write about sports?" He asked. His tone was partially sarcastic, partially antagonistic. That wasn't part of the preplanned conversation, though it probably should have been.

Audrey rolled her eyes. "I'm better than that."

"You absolutely are."

"Daddy, let me finish," she said, realizing she was about to be derailed.

He smiled apologetically. "I'm sorry, Audrey. Please go on. What's your new job?"

Taking a deep breath, she began. "I just got a call from a Mr. Tim Fleming, who is the public relations director for the Tigers. He wants me to be a new media intern." Saying it out loud made the true gravity of the situation hit her rather strongly. She not only had a new job. She had something of a dream job in her field, something that a few months ago she didn't think would ever happen.

Her father's eyes widened and he took a moment to respond. "Well, that does show our small minded newspaper boy, doesn't it?" He said proudly. "Writing for a real big league team?"

"Yeah. A real team. My team." She went over to him and they hugged each other tightly. Yet again, for a moment, everything seemed like it would be all right.

21

In her best suit, Audrey slipped into the Administration door. She had been panicking about this since she had received the phone call, but now with everyone in the lobby of the offices looking like they were staring at her, wondering what she was up to, she felt even more faint. Trying not to show any of that, she walked confidently up to the desk. "Hello, my name's Audrey Dawson," she said nervously to the man seated there.

He smiled. "Audrey Dawson. Heard a lot about you."

"You have?"

"Mr. Fleming's got everyone reading *This Urban Jungle.* You've certainly got a way with words for such a young lady."

Audrey blushed. "I'm not that young."

"Younger than me..." He gestured to his graying hair. "I'll buzz up Mr. Fleming. You can go ahead and have a seat over there."

With a nod, she hurried over to do just that There were a couple magazines sitting on the table nearby and she grabbed one at random, pretending to read it while really observing the sort of people that came through the office. She'd been to the park countless times; she'd never even known this area was here. "So next exposé is on the grounds keepers, huh?" asked a voice to her left.

Audrey immediately closed the magazine, saw that it was devoted to turf management, and blushed. "No...nothing of the sort." She stood up and, with all of the confidence that she could muster, held out a hand. "You must be Mr. Fleming. I'm Audrey Dawson."

He shook it with a wide toothy grin that clearly read 'I am in marketing.' The fact that he had the people-pleasing personality of a public relations professional was evident almost immediately upon seeing him. Though he also looked a little more on the nerdy side than she had expected, being a taller lanky man with glasses as opposed to a muscular former ball player like the kind she saw doing commentaries on ESPN. Admittedly, this difference made her a little less horrified. He looked more like a fellow human being. "Pleased to meet you. And please, call me Tim."

"Pleasure's all mine, Mr...Tim."

"The office is this way." He smirked a bit and started off toward the elevator, then added, "And don't be so nervous. I wouldn't have picked you if I didn't think you were a good writer."

"I didn't even apply for anything," Audrey admitted, feeling the words tumble out of her mouth. "You haven't even done a review of my portfolio."

"After what I read, I didn't have to. Now, come along, this way."

The office was on the second floor of the administration area and smaller than the office at the paper, but she didn't say anything about that. She had somehow landed a once in a million chance job. Everyone at the paper was almost certainly dreaming of something like this. "So...is there like a manual or something?" She asked, unsure of what to say.

Instead of answering her, he nodded to a tablet that was sitting on his desk. She also noticed he had a copy of *Lily of the Valley* by Balzac, but she wasn't about to mention that. He clearly meant more for her to notice the tablet. "Isn't it a beauty?"

"We certainly don't have those just lying around our office at school," she mused.

"I imagine not. It's my new toy, but you see, the thing is, the reason I got it, is because I wanted a way to engage with more people, broaden the reach of the organization, use new media technologies and all of that sort of thing." He paused and looked at her.

"Sounds ambitious," she said, knowing this was the appropriate place in the conversation to respond.

"Not necessarily. It wouldn't be at all if I had more staff. That's where you come in."

Audrey wasn't sure what to say. Everything about the whole incident was still so surreal. "Me?"

"When I read the piece you wrote about seizing the day and all that, I was inspired. And, then, when I realized how many people were reading your writing I knew you were the answer. I have to handle a lot things and I don't have time myself between dealing with promotions. I need someone else who has just as much passion for this game and this team, but is better with words."

It was startling to hear someone talk about people reading her writing though she wasn't sure why. She had been working on the paper since her freshman year at Wayne State; she knew that people read her writing, at least in passing, but for some reason the thought that people were reading a blog that she put together on her own without anyone's support or publicity or coattails to ride and that she was getting attention, especially attention of this sort, was amazing. "So you want me to?"

"Keep blogging, basically. A little more officially, of course, and manage our social media. Think you can handle that?"

It sounded like a dream job. "Of course I can."

"Good." He picked up the tablet carefully like it was a child. "Want a tour?"

"Oh, no need," she said honestly. "I've been here plenty of times. I know where just about everything is."

"Behind the scenes?" He suggested. She nodded eagerly and Mr. Fleming laughed. "Thought that'd change your mind. Follow me."

He led her around, first showing everything she had already seen countless times, but she didn't complain. Something different was catching her eye this time. She thought, perhaps, it was because she had this new job that everything seemed slightly different, but then she began to look closer. It wasn't just that she felt more confident, there genuinely was something about the place that looked different.

There wasn't going to be a game until later that evening. When she had arrived, with the exception of administration, the area had been mostly devoid of life, but now it seemed that there were people standing around, though Mr. Fleming seemed to completely ignore them. One of them, seeming to notice her looking, tipped a hat to her and it hit her that he was wearing a Red Sox uniform. "What sort of sacrilege is that?" she whispered to herself.

She heard him laugh and call to her. "Just 'cause they traded me doesn't mean I'm not allowed to care about my team, m'lady!"

Shocked, she hurried after Mr. Fleming. She didn't know what to do. There were more of them. They were everywhere. They weren't just in baseball uniforms either. There were men in suits, even a couple of women were interspersed. She didn't know what to make of it at all. Her head was spinning.

"Are you all right?" She suddenly heard Mr. Fleming asking.

Audrey nodded. "I'm sorry, I'm just trying to take in the fact that this is happening."

He nodded with a knowing smile. "Yeah, that happens sometimes. You need water? Something to eat?"

"I'm fine. Show me what's behind the scenes. I can handle it."

He laughed yet again at that. She liked that he laughed a lot. It made him seem more approachable and less frightening. "This way," he said, gesturing to another door. "Just follow my lead."

Audrey loved her new job. Those at the paper who knew about it were jealous, even Tyler, who she saw from time to time at the games with his press pass. It didn't bother her anymore. Today, she sat in the best seats she had ever had, writing up her next entry. The game was over and almost everyone had cleared the stands, but she was waiting until she had every word in her head done. She didn't want to forget a single phrase. Suddenly, a glove landed on the seat next to her. Startled, she looked up to see Armando Rhymes standing on the other side of the fence smirking at her. "Not getting any interviews today?" He challenged.

She shook her head. "I haven't tried yet. Haven't had the bug to do anything of the player interview sort."

He laughed. "I don't know...you quoted me pretty well."

"You saying I should go down there and try to talk to them?"

"You're press, you've got a badge, right?"

Audrey shrugged. It felt nerve-wrecking to approach the players. She still found it surreal that Armando was talking to her, even now. Even though she now worked for the team, they all still seemed otherworldly and unapproachable. "Yeah, I do."

"Don't be so shy then. I want to see an interview. I bet you'll do better than half those other schmucks."

"I'm not ready yet. I'm waiting for the right moment. The right person and the right play are going to come along to talk about. It'll happen."

He didn't want to call her a coward, but a sigh and shake of his head said it well enough. "Don't let it wait too long, okay, Dawson? Don't want to miss your chance." He turned and started away.

"Hey, Rhymes, don't forget your glove." She tossed it back toward him. He turned around and caught it easily, despite the awkward shape. "Can I ask you something?" She said then.

He shook his head immediately. "Me? Oh no, You can't interview me. I already gave you one. That'd be too easy."

"Not an interview, just one question."

He pretended to ponder this a moment and then nodded. "Shoot."

"Do you see them too?"

He paused, looking at her seriously. There was a recognition on his face that confirmed it, but he didn't seem to want to say. "Who?"

Audrey got the feeling that he knew exactly what she was talking about. "It depends, doesn't it?"

He nodded, confirming her suspicions. In a very quiet voice that she wasn't sure how she was able to hear, he said, "I don't always see them anymore. Not since I was a kid, but I always feel them."

"I'm not crazy?"

Armando smirked, but didn't say anything else. He merely hit his fist into his glove and dashed off the field. She rolled her eyes as he left. Sure he didn't admit it, but why would he? At least she knew now that she wasn't the only one.

22

Everything had settled into a nice rhythm for a little while. Audrey finally began to get the feeling that she had a future and that her life was falling into place. Unfortunately, it wasn't to last. She was on her way to the park one Friday evening and was somewhat excited because she had almost talked Vanessa into coming to the game with the promise of fireworks. It was then that her phone rang while she was in the car. Traffic was a bit on the heavy side and she knew better than to attempt to answer while driving, but the fact that someone had called her then was a little disconcerting. Despite being what she liked to call a reporter, her phone had never exactly rung off the hook.

With much trepidation, she took out the phone to check the messages after she parked the car.

"No need to be alarmed," her mother's voice began as it issued from the phone's speakers. "Please don't you be alarmed and don't you dare come home until after the game." A long paused followed. Audrey didn't like the sound of this at all. She was starting to feel sick to her stomach. "In fact, I shouldn't even be leaving this message."

"Mom! Get on with it!" Audrey hissed at her phone as she made her way through the crowds.

"I'm taking your father back into the hospital, doll. He's been having a hard time breathing all day and that could mean the pneumonia is back. We don't want to take any chances. It's probably nothing though, to be honest. I don't want you to worry...and I -definitely- don't want you leaving work before the game is over. Do you hear me? Do your job and then you can come by. We'll probably be back at the house by then. This really shouldn't take long at all." Her message ended abruptly without even her cursory "I love you, doll" which tended to end every phone conversation that they had together. It wasn't a good sign at all. Desperately, she hoped that the message had merely been cut off for being so long and not that she had been in that much of a hurry.

With fumbling fingers, she tried calling home again. There was no answer. Nor was there one on her mother's cell phone. That boded even worse. She started for her seat, but the crowd suddenly felt crushing. She had the overwhelming urge to cry and she didn't want to be seen. Especially not by all these children with their parents. Far less than anything did she want to see happy families with healthy parents right now. She turned away from her section and began looking.

She couldn't help the tears that had already started to fall. She felt ridiculous and trying to find a less crowded place to cry wasn't working. It was a Friday night game against the Yankees; there was nowhere to go that wasn't full of people already. The lines for the bathrooms were long and every single space was crammed full of people. This was a good thing. It was job security. She knew that, but seeing people everywhere was starting to make her hyperventilate. She needed to be alone to get this out. Finally, when she simply couldn't take it any longer, she sat on a picnic table in a courtyard and put her head in her hands, trying in vain to keep the tears from slipping out.

"Is everything all right?" An unfamiliar male voice asked.

Audrey didn't look up. In fact, it annoyed her a little. This was a fine time for people to suddenly take interest in the well-being of those around them. "I'm fine. I just need a minute."

"They told me to come see after you," he said, pushing a little. His tone was kind, and she appreciated that. She didn't bear him any ill will; she just wanted to be left alone.

"Really, I'm fine." He sat down next to her and instinctively, she moved away. "I said I'm fine. I just want to be left alone."

"Ma'am..."

She jumped to her feet, incredibly irritated by the intrusion. "Look, I don't know where you think-"

Abruptly, she cut off her sentence. Sitting there on the picnic bench was a tall, strong looking man in a 1930s Yankees uniform. She almost immediately recognized him as Lou Gehrig. "You..." she didn't mean to have such venom in her voice; she really didn't. It was just difficult not to when confronted with the man who's name had been infamously gifted to her father's illness. "What are you doing here? You don't belong here."

"I'm here with my team. I'm always with my team."

"That doesn't mean you get to come among the Tigers fans. Stay with the Yankees." Her voice was far more bitter than she meant it to be. Under different circumstances, she would have been in awe about meeting him, but right now it was just too much.

He nodded solemnly. "I'm sorry that you feel that way. I only meant to be of assistance."

"Can you cure him?" She challenged. Any other day and she would have regretted saying such a thing in anger, but she had already been pushed too far.

Lou shook his head. "No...no I can't."

"Then I don't want any assistance."

"I can help look after him, if you wish."

"He's dying. What good is it going to do to have someone around that he can't even see?"

Despite her angry and confrontational words, Lou seemed to remain incredibly calm. He merely nodded. "Is he a baseball man? Maybe he can see me."

That idea made Audrey pause a moment. She thought back to what Sam had said when she first met him, but then she shook her head. "You'll scare him even more than me."

"I didn't mean to scare you. You just looked so sad and everyone was worried."

"He'll think you're the angel of death."

"It was just an offer. One of your guys mentioned that you were pretty torn up about your father being sick and I figured, if there was anybody who should or could talk to you or him about it, it was me." He looked so sincere. Audrey was almost ready to forgive him for being a Yankee.

She still wasn't sure about accepting, however. Her father might not take it well. "Can you do that? Be in another city without the team?"

"I've never really tried," he said honestly. Audrey had to admit that particular fact suited everything she had learned about the dedicated man sitting at the table in front of her. "But since Detroit was...where it ended..."

The word ended made her tense up. She shook her head. "I couldn't ask you to do that. I sincerely couldn't."

"Maybe just a quick stop? He can think the whole thing is a dream."

"No...I couldn't..."

"It would mean a lot to me."

Audrey paused, still uncertain. What would it mean if she agreed? She didn't know what to do with all this. Still, after a long moment of consideration, she held out her hand. "Meet me after the game." He smiled a rather genuinely nice smile and then was gone.

It was then that Audrey noticed a huge crowd of people in the courtyard staring at her as though she had completely lost her mind. She had just been having a conversation with a person that most likely all of them couldn't see and if any of them could, they probably didn't believe what was going on in front of their eyes. A security guard stepped forward, but out of no where Mr. Fleming intercepted. "Miss Dawson, please come with me immediately," he said, talking her by the arm and leading her out of the courtyard. Her heart sank to her feet.

Mr. Fleming took her back up to the office. He looked incredibly uncertain about what to say and Audrey was convinced that he was about to fire her. "I can explain," she began after a few long tense minutes of silence.

He shook his head. "I just needed to get you out of there. Are you all right?"

"I really can explain."

"Is this about your father?"

Audrey knew that she hadn't mentioned anything about that to Mr. Fleming. In fact she had mentioned it to very few other people aside from Sam and that was only in passing when she went back to tell him that while there had been plenty of comments praising his on base percentage on her Balzac article, none of them seemed to be from the nerdy kid he was seeking. "Well..."

"If you want to go home, by all means, Miss Dawson, I understand," He said calmly. "This sort of thing is tough."

"You're not firing me?" She couldn't believe it.

"Why would I fire you?" He asked sincerely, shaking his head.

"Well, I was having a conversation with myself in front of a crowd of people for starters."

"People do that around here all the time. I try not to pass judgment."

"Staff?" She asked, slightly incredulous

Mr. Fleming took the copy of *Lily of the Valley* off his desk and held it out to her and nodded. "Of course, staff. Most of the time though, we try to keep those sorts of conversations in our offices."

She took the book uncertainly. Then after a long moment of staring at the cover, it clicked. "You're...the boy who reads Balzac?"

"When you wrote that article..." He shook his head, looking more than a little nostalgic. It was the look that the patrons of the coffee shop would get when she interviewed them about their first games. "I couldn't believe it."

"But...Sam said it would be a little boy following his brother."

"And it was. Thirty some years ago, anyway." Audrey stared, unsure of how to respond as he went on. "I'll never forget my first game, you know. I don't think anyone really does. My brother was watching me because my mother was working and he wanted to go see the Tigers play. I didn't, but he was bigger and I was a scrawny little thing, who was exceptionally easy to threaten. I took my book, planning to read the whole time. Let's just say for the sake of posterity, I didn't."

She nodded, turning the book over awkwardly in her hands. It looked well loved. "I'm not sure I entirely understand." Sam had only told her this a month or so ago. Had he been wrong about the date? Was there another boy that was supposed to be coming there that day? It didn't make any sense.

Mr. Fleming shook his head. "They're there. They're always there. It's the nature of the game. It echoes into the future."

Audrey didn't know what else to say. She still didn't quite understand what he meant specifically, but she agreed about the echoes. She paused a moment thinking of how to work that into another piece. At least it would keep her mind off her father until the game was over and she could get home. "If you don't mind, I think I'd like to get back to work."

"Of course," Mr. Fleming said with a nod. "Just try to keep an eye out? No more incidents?"

She nodded. "I'll be sure to."

23

Upon her arrival home, Audrey felt like the whole world around her was moving in slow motion. The family car was in the driveway, which she hoped meant that her parents were home. She didn't want to think about the possibility that it meant they had left in an ambulance.

"Mom? Dad?" She called as she slipped into the house. It was dark, but that still didn't mean anything. It was also late. She heard voices coming from the living room and, with care, started in that direction. "Daddy?"

"Audrey, come in here!" His voice was quite excited. It almost sounded like it used to years ago.

Still, she was hesitant. "Yes, Daddy?"

When she walked into the room, he was there, in the hospital bed as she had hoped and expected, but he was sitting up. In the chair nearby was Lou. Audrey had to smile at the look of childish joy on her father's face. "Who's this?" she asked, feigning ignorance.

"Audrey, I'm sure you recognize Mr. Gehrig," Her father said.

Lou stood up and nodded to her before sitting back down. "Mr. Dawson has been telling me a great deal about you He seems to be very pleased to have such an accomplished young woman for a daughter."

Audrey couldn't help blushing. "Daddy..."

"It's true," her father said. "This girl is the best thing in my life. I'm lucky."

Lou nodded toward him again. "I should be going, Mr. Dawson."

"No, " Audrey said immediately. "Please, stay. Don't let me get in the way."

"You're not in the way at all, Miss Dawson, I should just be going. Your father and I had a very good chat though, didn't we Reggie?"

"Once in a lifetime thing," he replied. "Best dream I ever had."

Audrey had missed that smile a great deal. It meant more than anything to see it again.

Her thoughts on her father, asleep downstairs and thinking that he had a dream about a visit from Lou Gehrig, seemed to be slowing the flow of ideas that night and Audrey stared blankly at her computer screen. Despite trying to focus, her mind was in so many other places that she simply couldn't making anything baseball related flow in the right way. Suddenly, though she didn't type anything, words began to appear on the screen of their own accord. "Need some help?" The blank document suddenly read.

Audrey shook her head, more out of shock than as a genuine refusal. "Excuse me?"

"Not that you need it, but I've got an idea for you," read the screen in response

"Who is this?" She asked in a very low whisper. No one was awake to overhear her, but one couldn't be too careful.

Again, the answer appeared on the screen. "Just an old sportscaster."

She spun around in her chair immediately, not waiting for anything more. When the man she saw standing there was wearing a Cleveland uniform, she was profoundly disappointed. The look showed very clearly on her face. "Who are you?" she asked, far less enthusiastic than she had been a moment ago.

"Don't look like that. I'm not a bad guy," he said in a clear broadcaster's voice. There was something unmistakable about that kind of voice.

Audrey blushed with embarrassment and attempted to apologize. "I'm sure you're not. I just - you weren't who I was expecting."

He nodded understandingly at that. "No. No, I imagine not, being a Tigers girl and all, but I need the exact right person for this job."

"I'm sorry, but...who are you?"

He smiled before answering. "Well, my name's Herb Score. Cleveland fan would have known that, but..." He glanced over his shoulder and sighed. He knew what she wanted, so he allowed the tone of his voice to turn conspiratorial. "He's here you know."

She didn't have time to react to the first bit of his statement. Her mind had latched onto the second. "What do you mean?"

"Exactly what you think I mean. He's here too. Been here with you awhile actually."

"What do you mean by that?" she repeated.

He kept going without really answering her question. "See, the thing is, he seems to have the idea that you're talented enough on your own that you don't need any assistance. Just a little bit of a guiding hand. One that's kept unseen, of course."

"What. Do. You. Mean?" Audrey was getting frustrated.

Herb shrugged. "He might be a little upset with me if I told you. He doesn't want to stifle your natural talent."

"He wouldn't. I promise he wouldn't."

"I'm just relaying what I've been told."

Audrey frowned and tried to look hard into all of the shadows, but it didn't seem that anyone else was there. "What's your idea?" She asked sounding very resigned and more than a little confused.

"Well," Herb began. "I've got a player that I think might be an interesting interview for you."

"-You've- got a player?"

He nodded. "Cleveland, actually. Cleveland will have a player in the near future."

"I write a blog about Detroit," she said, shaking her head.

"That is if they have the sense to snatch her up while they can."

"I write a Detroit Tigers blog," she protested again and then suddenly what he said clicked. "Did you say her?"

Herb nodded. "She's a pitcher. I have it on good authority that she's going to be pitching a game between the Lake County Captains and West Michigan Whitecaps next weekend as a bit of a side show promotion, novelty kind of thing, but I have a feeling that she's going to be a lot more impressive than they expect and you should be there. I think you should talk to her."

Audrey had to admit that the thought of a female ballplayer intrigued her a great deal. "What's her name?"

"Gioia Rinaldi."

Audrey repeated the name to herself. "It's next weekend? Just go down there?"

"She'll be expecting you, I think. I'll lay the groundwork."

"Thank you...Mr. Score..." She took a deep breath and careful turned back to her computer.

"He's here," Herb said again, echoing his earlier statements. "Don't you worry about that."

Audrey wasn't able to respond. She merely nodded. Words from her childhood were ringing in her ears. Words from as far back as she could remember. The words that had inspired her and brought her to journalism as a career. She thought back to what Sam had said, that the person who was meant to find her would. She nodded carefully and began writing again, words flowing with a more confident ease.

PART THREE: CENTRAL DIVISION

24

It was a rather gentle snowfall, not altogether atypical for Cleveland in the spring. Gioia had actually been expecting worse when it began, but it seemed like the lake effect winds were going to blow all of the nonsense east and beyond the city for once. The winds were more than enough to be a problem. They kept pushing against her, making it almost impossible to walk, let alone throw the ball she was clutching tightly in her fist.

She wasn't sure why she had set out on this little adventure, but she knew she had to do it. College had turned out to be everything she had hoped it wouldn't. "Treasure the friends you make in the first week. They'll be the ones to stick with you for the rest of your four years," read the guidebook for Introduction of University Life, the most depressing blow off course in existence. Gioia, however, didn't make friends that first week, or the first month, or the first few months. She had gone home for Christmas to hear tales from her friends about parties and adventures all over the state: in Athens, in Gambier, in Westerville, in Upper Arlington, even in such far flung places as Houghton, Michigan and New York City. She didn't have any stories of her own to share. She made up a few, but they were nothing like everyone else's, and she had never been a particularly good liar. The truth was, none of the girls in her dorm would talk to her and she wasn't finding it terribly easy to make friends. None of that was too different than high school, but at least in high school she had softball to keep her mind off of things. She had also been able to cultivate a friend or two over the years. She wrote to Nellie, but as the year wore on her best friend's replies became increasingly shorter and more infrequent. She was never on any instant messengers. Now that Gioia was in college she had to start all over and she had no idea where to begin.

It was already April. The first year was about to end and she hadn't made a single friend. This had to be fixed or she didn't know if she would be able to bring herself to come back to Cleveland State for another year. She had to come up with a reason to stay, so she took out her bus pass and set out on an adventure that was probably a horrible idea. She set out to find League Park.

She knew vaguely where it was and that it was still standing. She had hoped, perhaps naively, that if she got there, Cy would come back, maybe even some others. That was the original home of a lot of baseball ghosts after all. If she got lucky she would have someone to talk to again. Even if they were just baseball ghosts, they were still more intellectually stimulating than her completely noncommunicative roommate, Nikki, who refused to even ask Gioia to turn down music, or to share her pizza, or take out the trash, all things Gioia felt would be typical roommate requests. Listening to music didn't quell the crushing loneliness of the silence anymore. She had to deal with it and she had to deal with it fast.

League Park had been easier to find than she had expected. Modern technology could be a bit of a wonder sometimes. So she sat on the mound in the middle of the empty park, watching the spring snow fall all around her as she hoped for some spirit to appear. They'd come before. They had to come again.

She squeezed her eyes tightly shut, trying to picture the old field back home at Tusky Valley. Maybe if she thought of the place where Cy had first appeared it would be easier to call him to her.

"Young lady, what do you think you're doing? You're going to catch your death!" a female voice shouted.

Gioia squeezed her eyes tighter. She didn't want to deal with someone real right now.

"Young lady, don't make me start sounding like my mother!"

With a sigh, Gioia opened her eyes. What she saw was far from what she had expected. She was right about the fact that the voice was female, but she was wrong about everything else. Gioia had to admit that though she had heard of them, she had never actually seen a woman wearing bloomers before. "Who are you?"

"Were you expecting someone else?" she asked, smirking and walking out to the mound. She had a baseball in her hand as well.

"Well, last time, Cy..."

"Cy! Very nice, very nice. He doesn't like to show up much. I think he might have a bit of an ego, award named after him and all."

"He...said it was closer to home."

She smiled. There was something nostalgic about it. "That's something he and I have in common. Aside from the pitching of course."

"You're home here?"

She shook her head. "Not technically. I mean, I only like to go home. I prefer home. Haven't been there in ages."

"There? Not here?"

"This is my home field...but no...My home is Ragersville."

"That's not far from me at all!" Gioia couldn't help exclaiming.

"You're not from Cleveland?"

"I'm from Bolivar!" She said excitedly.

The woman laughed and sounded a bit like Nellie when she did. Gioia had missed that. "We're practically neighbors. What's your name then?"

Gioia finally stood up and held out her hand. "Gioia Rinaldi, and I'm sad to say I've probably never heard of you. I know every ball player from Ohio. I kept a list when I was younger. They were only men."

"My name's Alta Weiss," she said, shaking Gioia's outstretched hand. "and I'm unfortunately not terribly surprised. I didn't get as far as I would have liked."

"Bloomers?" Gioia couldn't help asking. Even the girls in *A League of Their Own* had worn skirts and that looked to have certainly been set in a time after when Alta had played.

Alta laughed again. "Yes, bloomers. They're surprisingly versatile. You'll break your neck in a skirt...people quote me on that."

"I find pants more versatile," Gioia teased. She felt her old self slowly coming back to her. She finally had someone she could talk to. Someone who knew what it was like to be who she was, to want what she wanted, to have the disappointments that she had.

"I don't think you should be so quick to dismiss your elders, young lady. It's because I needed to wear bloomers to play baseball or ride a bike that you get the option of wearing pants."

"My elders?" Gioia asked smirking. "I thought you didn't want to sound like your mother."

"How do you know my mother said anything of the sort?"

Gioia shrugged a little. "Mine would. Sometimes she might be joking, but she'd say it."

"Sounds like I'd get along with your mother."

"She's a good woman..." Gioia paused a moment, feeling silly, but something had just occurred to her. "um, Alta?"

"Yes?"

"I was thinking of maybe going to a game today..." She felt terribly silly asking, especially because she didn't know how these ghost things worked. Cy had only once shown himself off the field, but he talked like he had gone to other places before. "I've been wanting to for awhile. It's just I feel really silly going alone..."

Alta smiled indulgently. "No one else can see me, you know. People will still think that you're alone."

"Maybe," Gioia said with a small shrug. "But I'll know I'm not."

"Then I'll go with you. Just don't be surprised when they think you're talking to yourself."

It seemed weird to get off the bus at 9th street and walk in from that direction. All of these years she had been taking the RTA to the station under Tower City. She felt displaced and turned around as she walked through the crowds of street vendors selling peanuts and t-shirts. They didn't seem to mind the fact that it was still wintery cold in Cleveland in April, though she imagined the trade in jackets was a bit more brisk than that in t-shirts. "Come snow or mayflys," she said happily to herself as the ball park came into view.

"Mayflys" Alta shuddered at that.

"Don't knock them. Mayflys almost won us an American League Championship. They took out the Yankees rather handily."

"And it was a dirty trick then as much as it would be now."

"Trick?"

"I give Nap credit though. He stands up for his team. The Yankee boys are always pulling things on everyone else: influencing the game, moving balls about, messing around. We do have to fight back every once and awhile."

Gioia mulled this over and the only conclusion that she could draw from it was slightly disconcerting. Ever since she saw the series of players looking after her brother, she had known that there were more baseball ghosts in the world and it wasn't a leap of imagination to think that every team must have their own set of them hanging around, but influencing the game seemed a little too *Angels in the Outfield* for her tastes. "You know, I don't think I want to know what you mean by that."

Alta laughed. "Smart girl."

As Alta appeared to be watching a group of men standing around the gates to the cemetery across the street, Gioia went up and bought her ticket. "Shouldn't you be in school?" The man at the ticket window asked, laughing a bit.

Gioia shook her head, knowing he thought she was a high school student. People often did. "That's the glory of college, sir."

He nodded and passed over a ticket with a smile. It was a nice cheap seat out in the right field triangle. She was more used to the bleacher seats, but it just felt wrong sitting there without Marco and her parents. Besides people rarely sat out in right field; she'd be able to talk to Alta without anyone thinking she was in need of institutionalization. She looked over in Alta's direction. Her new friend was still watching the graveyard with a weird expression. She wanted to ask about it, but there were too many people around.

Eventually, her bloomers wearing ghost turned back around and started to walk with her. "Something's happening," was all she said. Gioia knew better than to react, but it was all that she could do to stop herself.

As they started up to their seats, the smell of hotdogs and pierogi was simply intoxicating. Her stomach was growling a little, but Gioia wasn't sure of the proper protocol when it came to eating around ghosts. Was it offensive? She glanced at Alta and marveled momentarily at her ability to weave through crowds that weren't even able to see her.

Alta looked at her knowingly. "If you want a hotdog, I'm not going to object."

"Are you sure?" she whispered, looking around to make sure no one was listening.

She nodded and Gioia hurried over to the line. One hotdog and spicy mustard. The man next to her laughed. "Shouldn't you be in school, young lady?"

Gioia bristled, offended slightly because so many people seemed to think she was younger than she was, but she was in a good mood today and tried to shake it off. "Don't tell me that you've never skipped class for a baseball game," she said instead.

The man laughed. "Plenty of times. This team made me into quite the little truant when I was young."

"Some things never change..."

"It was easier to hide in municipal though. All that scaffolding."

Gioia laughed. She had only the vaguest memories of that particular stadium, now long gone. Memories of the sort that in all honesty, she wasn't entirely sure if they were her own or if she had simply seen photographs and created them in her mind.

"Win more here, though," he mused. "Not that you can convince people of that..."

She wasn't sure if she wanted to engage in a statistics discussion with a stranger as much as she wanted to try. "I reserve judgment," was all she said in response.

"We live in a city stuffed to the gills with pessimists," he replied, dropping a large amount of onions on top of the hotdog.

It wasn't too hard for Gioia to believe his words. Technically, though she'd never admit it, she was one of them. There was a lot to be pessimistic about in Ohio these days that had absolutely nothing to do with baseball. It made a lot of sense that some of that pessimism would bleed over. "I prefer to err on the side of persistence myself," she said instead. "Gotta get up the next day, keep going. Maybe you'll get a break." This was something of a lie. In her mind, she knew that the two were not mutually exclusive: one could easily be persistent while still feeling like there wasn't anything worthwhile in their future. She knew this because that was increasingly becoming her own outlook on life. Still, it wasn't polite to have conversations like that with a complete stranger, and especially not in a ball park. The ball park was a sacred space to get away from all those feelings.

He nodded approvingly at her statement. "It'll happen again one day, mark my words," he said before walking away.

Gioia, hotdog in hand, hurried back to Alta and they up continued up to their seats. Once they had cleared the rather bored looking usher and taken their place in the awkward triangular section of seats, Gioia finally asked. "What were you watching down at the gate?"

Alta shook her head. "It's not important."

"You looked concerned about something in the graveyard."

"Not concerned, just curious."

"About?" Gioia pushed, curious herself.

"It's a beyond the scenes thing, Gioia, for us superstitious folk. I don't think I should tell you yet."

Squinting her eyes at the field, she shook her head. "I'm superstitious too. It's hard not to be."

"Yes, but..." She smiled. "There were ghosts."

"Baseball's full of ghosts." Her tone was teasing. That was something her father had told her since she was a little girl. She'd always believed it, but not as literally has she had come to in the past year.

Alta didn't take the bait, she merely nodded with an indulgent smile. " When so many people love a game so much, it's hard for there not to be ghosts. Places have energy, Gioia."

She supposed that was true and was about to voice that when a triple play ended the inning. Her eyes widened. This looked like it was going to be a rather different game than what she had grown used to.

25

It was difficult for Gioia to focus in her classes during the following weeks. Particularly because all through her Principles of Macroeconomics lecture, someone had a baseball game pulled up on their laptop one row ahead. Though she was trying her best to focus on her professor's words regarding the international monetary system, her eyes kept floating back in that direction. It was almost like some sort of baseball magnet.

"Miss Rinaldi," she heard suddenly from the front of the room, when she had been staring at it for a particularly long time. There had been a very impressive behind the back throw by her favorite shortstop.

She looked up, deeply concerned. "Yes, sir?"

Her professor rolled his eyes. "What can you tell us about money supply controls?"

Panicked, she flipped forward a few pages in her notes, which she had neglected to do, distracted as she was by the game. "The...the basic principles of...monetary controls..."

Again her professor rolled his eyes. "That will be all, Miss Rinaldi. I know that the back of Mr. Hattori's head must be fascinating, but the rest of us are here to study macroeconomics. Now if perhaps Mr. Kennan would like to give it a try."

Gioia turned several different shades of red as the boy in front of her who's laptop had been displaying the baseball game, now identified as Mr. Hattori, turned around to look at her. She shook her head and mouthed "Baseball game." He pointed at the screen and smiled, before turning back to watch Cleveland's next at bat.

After class, she hurried to pack up, hoping that her professor would not come back and reprimand her for daydreaming. She felt bad enough about it already. Unfortunately, she wasn't fast enough for as she carefully tucked her books into her bag, the boy with the laptop walked up to her. "Hey...sorry about that."

She shook her head. It wasn't his fault. "I shouldn't have been watching..."

"But did you see that play?" He asked excitedly.

"The behind the back throw? I knew there was a reason I liked him."

"He's been doing a lot better this year."

Gioia nodded. "They all have. It's encouraging actually."

"I love them either way. It's the nature of the beast, right?"

"Tell me about it," She said with another laugh, so happy to be talking baseball with a living person. "I don't think I could ever have a different favorite team, no matter how long it takes to win another World Series."

"Me either."

As they talked, the professor walked by and shook his head. "Ah, young love. Just make sure to keep it out of the classroom for now."

Gioia rolled her eyes and ignored him. When the professor had left, she frowned and looked apologetically to her new acquaintance. "No offense to you or anything, but I really was just watching the baseball game."

"None taken. My name's Daisuki by the way. You don't have to call me Mr. Hattori."

"Gioia." she held out her hand and he shook it awkwardly. "What's wrong?" She asked.

He just laughed. "That's just so formal, shaking hands. We could just be friends instead of business associates, you know."

Gioia laughed, feeling rather embarrassed. "Sorry."

"Don't worry about it."

She slung her book bag over her shoulder. "Thanks for letting me watch the game."

"Anytime. Maybe even some time when there's not an economics lecture happening around it."

"Sure, have you ever been in person?" She felt ridiculous immediately after she asked that. Of course he had, he was living in Cleveland. A baseball fan couldn't go too long without a live game.

He laughed a little. "Maybe only a million times, but I'm willing to make it a million and one."

"They're in Kansas City this weekend, but maybe after that?" She suggested without even thinking about it.

"You know the schedule by heart?"

She blushed at the incredulity in Daisuki's tone. She did, in fact. "I have a lot of spare time."

"Who are they playing next Saturday?" he challenged.

"Seattle."

"Home or Away?"

"Home."

"Then the Seattle game next Saturday it is. I still have a grudge against the Mariners, so..."

"I'll see you then." She hurried out of the classroom before realizing that she hadn't exactly given him any way to contact her.

It all worked out in the end. There was still another Macroeconomics class in between that moment and the game. They met outside Fenn Tower and caught a bus the rest of the way. It still felt awkward to Gioia, but at least she could see a nicely sized crowd as they made their way toward Progressive Field. "Seems like more people than last time," Gioia commented vaguely. It made sense. The last time she had gone with Alta had been a day game, most people were likely at work, however, it did feel like the crowd had increased by an amount even greater than that.

"Well, they're winning," Daisuki said. "They've got a nice streak going on."

Gioia understood that too, but it felt a touch disingenuous. "I wish people would come no matter what. I'd be here every day if I could."

"Not everyone's so dedicated."

"Says the boy who was watching the game in class."

Daisuki shook his head. "In my defense it was a really dry lecture."

They went to their seats and this time the ushers seemed to look a little less bored. "What do you think we'll be witness to today?" Gioia asked, trying not to be so awkward. At least baseball was a subject that she could talk about more naturally than most others.

"With these two teams, there's no telling what could happen." He pondered a moment, trying to come up with something spectacular. "Two grand slams. One game. Same hitter."

"Seattle or Cleveland?"

"For our sake let's hope Cleveland."

The team took the field and the game went well. There was no heavy scoring innings, nothing extraordinary, average baseball, but that didn't matter. It was still baseball. "So..." Daisuki began during a change between innings. "What got you into baseball?"

The worst non-baseball related subject Gioia had was talking about herself. She just shrugged. "Always have been. What about you?"

"Same. I played when I was younger. I hated it then; I kind of miss it now."

"You hated it?" Gioia couldn't imagine such blasphemy. Playing ball was the only real emotional release she ever had.

Daisuki looked away a minute and then continued. "My dad, he had this thing about forcing me to be more masculine. When I was a kid, I wanted to take ballet, and he kind of lost it. Since that was his reason for having me play, I didn't want to. I hated every minute on principle and I didn't even want him to know I enjoyed watching the games because he would take it as some sort of 'becoming a man' nonsense."

Gioia thought back to the taunting she had gotten for playing softball. It still hurt to think about it. Some part of her figured that it always would, even though most of those people probably didn't even remember her name anymore. "I kind of know what you mean."

"Really?"

"I played all through school. It's...a different sort of expectation for girls who play."

"I can imagine." Daisuki said. After a long pause, he attempted to lighten the mood. "Now, being away from all that, I do kind of find myself missing it. I wish we had a team. At the very least, it's be good to get some outdoor exercise. Can't exactly go running around campus."

"We have a softball team," Gioia said as a suggestion. She tried not to think about it herself. They had never shown interest in her and that hurt, so the best thing she could do for her sanity was to push it from her mind.

"Well, I doubt I'd be good enough anyway."

"Or me." Then, almost as if an answer to her wishes, the image of League Park floated into her mind. "No one said we can't play pick up games though."

"Where exactly?"

Gioia smirked mischievously. "Old League Park. I've been down there. They keep it. I think for little league or something, but I've been there."

Daisuki laughed a bit at her enthusiasm. "We'd need more than two people for a pick up game."

"We can find them, but until then." She shrugged. "When I was in high school I used to practice by myself. Two people is a definite improvement."

"I say you're crazy, but what the hell, I'm in." Just as he said the words, Cleveland's batter hit a single to load the bases. They both held their breath as the team's best slugger came up, waiting for the first of those grand slams Daisuki had predicted.

26

At first it was just the two of them going down to the field. Alta and a variety of other old Cleveland players showed up from time to time and got into the game, but Gioia wasn't entirely sure if Daisuki could see them or not. He never questioned when Gioia threw to what might have seemed to be empty voids of space, but he never threw to them himself either.

Eventually, other living people started to join in the game as well. There were a couple of kids from the area colleges, a few students who were clearly still in high school, the remnants of an old men's team that used to be affiliated with a now defunct paper plant and other remnants from a church league. With no one else to play, they did battle with each other. It was a rag tag bunch, but everyone seemed to be enjoying themselves a great deal and that was what truly mattered.

They even started attracting crowds and even more than one human interest story for various other local

Cleveland blogs. A lot of these stories praised Gioia's pitching abilities, though she herself was trying to ignore them.

"Pitcher, Cleveland State freshman, Gioia Rinaldi has to be one of the most superb young pitchers in the United States today," Paul, one of the older gentlemen read to a group made up of both his teammates and baseball ghosts. She kept trying to hide her face as a serious blush was growing. "The scouting team for Cleveland baseball should take note before someone else does. There is no doubt in our minds that the next Cy Young award winner is playing pick up ball on weekends at League Park." He smiled proudly. "That's some high praise, Miss Rinaldi."

"Empty praise," Gioia said with a shrug. "And buried on page six. No one even reads that part. Unless you like polo."

"Don't be so modest, Gioia," Daisuki said with a laugh. "Take what you can get. Press is press."

Gioia shook her head. She didn't care about any of that right now. She had, despite everything that she told her parents, begun to resign herself to the possibility that maybe dreams didn't come true. "Are we going to play or are we just going to stand around here talking?"

With minimal muttering, the group took up their gloves and bats and went to begin the game. It was then that Gioia happened to notice a set of ghosts standing near the fence. Alta and Cy were at the front of the group, which seemed to be rather larger than she had expected. Standing with them, though, were two people whose names she couldn't quite place. One had on a Cleveland uniform that looked to have been dated from the 1950s. The other was clearly decked out in Detroit regalia. She wasn't sure what to make of that. She had disliked those old English Ds ever since she had been a young girl and they had been representative of Dover, one of the other local high schools.

She looked at them, wondering if they wanted her to come over, but both Alta and Cy shook their heads at once. "Play the game," Alta said. "We want them to see what you can do." She wasn't sure what to make of that, but she accepted the challenge.

The group's game was a fun little dance, as always. Daisuki made a great diving catch in left field. Paul managed to hit his first home run in the time that they had all been playing together. He claimed it was the first home run of his life. Gioia did well too. She didn't think it was particularly good, but the gaggle of ghosts appeared to be impressed.

When the others had gone on their way, Gioia finally approached the group. "So what's all this then?" She inquired.

"We wanted to show off the home town girl," Cy said.

It had been a long time since Gioia had seen him and she couldn't help but smile. "You brought a Detroit guy?"

Alta smirked, nudging him. "And you didn't think she would notice..."

"There have been plenty of trades over the years. The two teams have a lot of overlap."

Someone in the group laughed and added sarcastically, "got a lot of overlap with everyone these days..."

"What are you two up to?" Gioia asked, interrupting the impending argument.

Alta and Cy looked at each other for a moment and then she began carefully. "He's got the ear of some scouts."

Gioia didn't quite believe what she was hearing. "What do you mean?"

"I mean...after he played for Detroit, he was a scout for Cleveland. There's still some people who listen to what he has to say."

That struck hard. She knew that her two mentors expected her to jump into the air with sudden giddiness, but she couldn't bring herself to do so. "I'm sorry, but no," was her only response. It was the only thing that she could make herself say after such a statement.

Cy frowned. "Gioia. You're a very talented girl."

"No. I'm not letting you get my hopes up again. No more of this." She had been burned too much. Now that she had finally accepted that it was all over for her baseball career, she didn't want any more false hopes pushed in her face. She reached down, picked up her glove, and marched off the field.

27

The next night after class, Gioia went back to her room in Fenn Tower. Her noncommunicative roommate, Nikki, was sitting in the common area, reading. Not wanting to disturb her, Gioia attempted to slip past. The attempt was thwarted, however, when her phone began ringing halfway to the beds. Nikki looked up, something akin to rage in her eyes. Gioia tried to look apologetic as she rushed over to the beds to answer. "Hello?" she asked timidly.

"Gioia! Gioia, I have news and you can't tell anyone," her brother's excited voice said on the other line. He sounded like he would burst through the phone and hug her if he could.

"Marco?" she asked, somewhat shocked. The call seemed very out of the blue for him. "Is that you?"

"Of course it's me, who else does it sound like?"

She glanced warily back at Nikki who seemed to be ignoring her rather well now. Still she didn't want to disturb her. "What is it?" She whispered.

"Is your roommate sleeping or something?"

"Marco what is it?"

"You have to keep this a secret, okay, Gioia? You can't tell anyone. Not even Madre and Padre. Not yet. I want to surprise them."

"Sure, whatever you say. Just tell me what's going on?"

"I just heard. Clarke hurt his leg playing Dance Dance Revolution. They're calling me up tomorrow. I get to play!"

"Marco! That's incredible!" She couldn't help exclaiming; Nikki or no Nikki. It didn't matter, her brother was going to be playing in a major league game.

"I know right?! I still can't believe this is happening."

"Tomorrow?"

"Yeah. Please be there?"

"I wouldn't miss it for world. Are you kidding?"

"I'll have seats for you and the parents at will call. Don't tell them anything. If they ask, say you bought them."

"I'll do that," Gioia said. Despite the twinge of bitter jealousy, which she couldn't really help, she felt happy for her brother. "Congratulations, Marco."

"Thanks, Gioia." When she heard the click on the other end, she hung up the phone and spun around excitedly.

It was then that Nikki spoke the first words that she had all year. "Got a date or something?" She asked, sounding more irritated than genuinely curious.

Gioia was quite shocked, but she shook her head. "No. My brother's going to play outfield in the majors."

Nikki puzzled over that a moment before shrugging and going back to watching TV.

The next night, Gioia met her parents at the gate. They looked like they knew why they had all been summoned there, but they pretended not to have any sort of clue. "Marco can be so mysterious sometimes," Mr. Rinaldi said, smirking at his daughter when she met them at the gate.

"You know?" She asked carefully, looking around as though Marco would suddenly appear to reprimand her or worse: say it was all a joke.

He shook his head. "I have absolutely no idea what you're talking about."

"Of course you don't," she muttered as the three of them made their way to their seats in the bleachers and listened with rapt attention as one Marco Rinaldi was announced as the left fielder.

"He's so young," Mr. Rinaldi said. There was pride in his voice, but also concern.

"That's my boy!" Mrs. Rinaldi said instead.

Gioia was speechless.

None of them left their seats the whole game. Not even Mr. Rinaldi went to get his customary spicy peanuts. They all had their eyes locked on Marco. Cleveland was doing very well that game and Marco, individually, was playing adequately. Gioia could tell he was nervous. There were a couple of plays he should have made that he didn't, but otherwise all seemed to be well. His hitting wasn't bad either. He struck out once, but proceeded to get a hit the next two times at bat. They all knew that it wouldn't last. As soon as Clarke's leg had healed, Marco would be back off to Akron or Columbus, but for now, they reveled in it.

Unfortunately, in the eighth inning a fly ball got away from him, allowing an unnecessary run. The entire Rinaldi family cringed in unison. "That's all anyone will remember," Mrs. Rinaldi said sadly, shaking her head.

And she was right. Even though Cleveland ended up winning the game 6-5, all anyone could talk about in the restaurant afterward was the rookie who dropped the ball. Mr. Rinaldi shook his head when he took his seat at their table after they had finally been seated. "Marco's not going to like all this, maybe we should find a different restaurant."

Mrs. Rinaldi grudgingly nodded. "If you can get a hold of him, ask him what he wants."

"Too late, Madre," Gioia said as she glanced toward the door and saw her brother standing there, looking tired and still shaking from residual nerves.

"Oh, my baby, Marco..." Mrs. Rinaldi said with loving sadness as got up and gestured to him.

Marco wadded through the crowd of people and started to his family's table. Conversations all around the restaurant stopped as they laid eyes on him. He sat down and Gioia reached over automatically to take his arm. "Marco..." she began.

"I don't want to talk about it," Marco said immediately.

Mrs. Rinaldi shook her head. "You did great. That's all I'll say on the matter."

Mr. Rinaldi shook his head as well, adding at the exact same time as his wife, "fine game, Marco. A fine game."

Marco finally looked to his sister. "And what about you? Gonna give me some false praise too?"

Gioia shook her head and said matter of factly, "you dropped the ball and the guy on second scored, when it should have been the third out of the inning." Both of the Rinaldi parents looked at their daughter as though she had grown a third head. It wasn't appropriate to say it so bluntly, even if it was true.

Marco, however, seemed to appreciate her honesty. "Thank you, Gioia. I'm glad at least one person in this family can be honest with me."

"But," Gioia interjected in a very businesslike tone. "If you think that dropping that ball means that you didn't play a good game or that it cancels out everything you did, like that beautiful line drive in the fourth inning, well, then you're just pitying yourself."

The whole family sat in stunned silence. "I am not," Marco finally said after a full minute, sounding rather offended.

"You are. You're twenty. You're a baby. They were testing you out."

"And I failed."

"You'd get a solid C from me. C's are average. Average isn't bad."

He wasn't sure how to react to what his sister was saying. He had expected and appreciated an honest answer from her, but there was something about her words and tone. The confidence seemed so strange coming from someone who fussed over her performance just as much as she did. Something about her manner was changed. She was more mature. "Gioia...I don't..."

"You'll get better." She shrugged. Both of their parents were still watching the exchange with partially concerned, partially confused, expressions.

Marco shook his head. "Doesn't matter. Soon as Clarke is better, they'll send me down again."

"You already knew that though. Clarke's a star."

"I suppose, but..." Marco trailed off, trying to think of an appropriate comeback, but he couldn't. "I don't know what to do with this."

"You in the line up tomorrow?"

"I don't know that yet."

"Well, if you are...that's another shot. Tomorrow's another day. Today's already gone."

"That's very wise, Gioia," her father said with a nod, agreeing but trying to shut down the conversation all the same.

Marco shook his head and gestured toward the people surrounding them at the restaurant. "Not to them."

Gioia sighed and looked out at the crowd. "Maybe, but now it's your job to change their minds."

28

That weekend, the group gathered to play another game at League Park. It was probably the last Gioia would be able to get to for awhile, as summer was coming on fast. Many of the people she played with lived in the area so it wasn't hard for them to continue, but she would have to get back to Bolivar for the summer and hopefully, with a great deal of luck, find a part time waitressing job. For the occasion, they had all decided to pitch in a few dollars and bring in a spread from a place in Little Italy. Everyone had been quite enthusiastic when Paul suggested the idea, merely because Paul was so convincing with his speech.

Gioia sat on the outfield grass, enjoying a slice of artichoke pizza, when Daisuki pointed to a man in a suit who was approaching, he looked grimly serious and stood almost half in shadow. "Looks like we've got the

FBI to contend with. Should have known better than to hang around with you," he teased.

Gioia slapped his arm playfully. "Shut up." She rolled her eyes and went back to her pizza. There was a nice little memory in that as well, something drawing her back to her mother's kitchen.

"Excuse me, is there a Miss Rinaldi here?" an unfamiliar voice asked, interrupting the festivities.

Gioia and Daisuki shared a look, half of amusement, but also half of genuine concern. She swallowed the last bite of her pizza and stood up. "That would be me."

The man in the suit walked over to the fence. "I'm supposed to come see you play."

"Not in order to arrest me, I hope," she said nervously, trying to tease for Daisuki's sake.

The man in the suit smirked a bit at that. "Who do you think I am?"

"We don't really have any idea," Gioia said with a shrug. The rest of the team had crowded around to listen to the exchange.

He looked over the whole group and nodded slowly. "Well, I came down here today to see an amateur baseball contest."

"Did you?"

He nodded slowly. "A voice on the wind might have told me that this girl, Gioia Rinaldi, was something to see; a force to be reckoned with, I believe were the exact words he used."

Everyone in the group looked at Gioia and each other cautiously. Sure people had come to watch before, but there was something strange about this man. He seemed far more businesslike than anyone else who had ever come by the park. Daisuki spoke up first. "Sure, you're welcome to watch."

"Daisuki," Gioia hissed, unsure of what to say. He was here specifically for her and that bothered her a bit.

"Don't be shy, Gioia," Paul interjected. "We were going to play here soon as we ate, anyway."

She still wasn't sure, but she nodded. "Fine...fine...but you have to let us finish eating first."

Paul gestured to the fold out table. "Grab a bite. It's from Presti's."

The suited man smiled appreciatively. "Don't mind if I do."

"Traitors, all of you," Gioia muttered to herself.

It wasn't long before the whole group agreed they were done eating and ready to take the field. Gioia did so grudgingly, but they all knew she wasn't going to play any less than her best. It was almost impossible for her once she got into the rhythm of the game.

Gioia tried to ignore the man who was standing just off to the side of third base, munching on pull apart bread and grinning like he had just unearth buried treasure. She used as much mental energy as she could not to let her thoughts drift back to her high school games and what had happened there. She didn't want to get her hopes up about anything, for all she knew this man was an escaped convict. She merely closed her eyes, shut out the world, and tried to keep in the game among the friends who she had grown to love.

After the game the whole group congratulated each other and made plans to meet a few times over the course of the summer. Gioia and Daisuki stood to the side as they did so. "Gonna miss it?" Daisuki asked.

"You know I will. It's my one release," she said a twinge of sadness in her voice though she was trying to force such thoughts away.

"So will I." The same sadness seemed evident in his voice.

A thought suddenly came into her mind. "Did you ever get to take ballet?" Gioia couldn't help asking, remembering what they had discussed when they first went to the Cleveland game together.

Daisuki shook his head. "My dad would have never allowed that."

"Your fielding is very dance like," Gioia suggested, trying to sound encouraging.

He laughed. "Maybe I would have been great."

"Well, you're a good fielder at the very least."

Again, he laughed. "Whatever you say."

The man at the fence fake coughed loudly just then. Both Gioia and Daisuki turned to him. "I don't mean to interrupt, I was just hoping to chat with you before it got dark."

Gioia looked to all of her friends as if to say '*If he attacks, you know how to use those bats*', and walked over. "Yes? What is this about?"

"So defensive, you are."

"I'm sorry. You showed up out of the blue. Forgive me for being a touch suspicious."

He shrugged slightly. "I honestly figured that you would have been expecting this to happen for awhile."

Gioia raised a skeptical eyebrow. "Expecting what?"

"A visit from a scout."

As that statement hit her, Gioia had to choke back a laugh. "A what?"

"A scout. A baseball scout."

"You're kidding, right?"

"Not even slightly." He held out his card, which she took, still feeling suspicious. "My name's Peter Sullivan. I've been in this business for a long time."

"Sure you have." She looked the card over carefully. Everything about it seemed legitimate, but nowadays it was quite easy to create a fraudulent business card.

"Look," Peter said carefully. "I've been hearing a lot about you. I just thought I'd stop by and give all the rumors a checking on. If you were half as good as they say you are, I figured maybe you'd want to come pitch a game with the Lake County Captains."

"Captains? They're like...single A, right?"

Peter nodded. "I don't think I'd be able to get a female pitcher in a higher level at the moment, but hey, if you're all right, you never know where you could end up."

Part of Gioia wanted to jump at the chance immediately. This was the part of her that still hadn't let go of her dreams. The slightly more sensible and definitely more cynical part of her still didn't believe this sort of thing could possibly be happening. There had to be a catch. She nodded slowly, still looking over the card. "It sounds like quite the opportunity."

"It truly is."

"And what's in it for you?"

"What?" He looked taken aback.

"Why would you come all this way for me? There's plenty of great players out there to snatch up. The world isn't exactly devoid of people who want to play baseball." She tried to ignore the fact that her team, who were mostly eavesdropping on the conversation, all groaned at that.

He seemed to consider this a moment. "You're shrewd. I'll give you that. I was expecting a starry eyed kid."

"I love baseball. That doesn't make me naïve."

"Well, you -are- Cleveland fan."

"There's that, but that makes me a believer, not naïve."

They both considered each other a moment, before Peter finally relented. "I want a girl pitcher. I heard about you and I was thinking that the novelty might be a good draw. Figured it might bring in a crowd."

"A crowd?" Gioia had to smirk at that. She didn't know if she wanted to draw a crowd. Deep down, part of her did. That was the part that still dreamed of a stadium full of fans cheering on her and her team. There was another part, however, that simply could not get behind that idea. That part remembered the sort of things that had happened when she started getting more attention for her softball playing back in high school. That had not been what she had dreamed of. The jeering had hurt.

"People like a good dose of something new. It helps get them in seats for the minor league games. We've never had as big of a draw."

Gioia remembered Marco. She remembered him complaining about how the players who had already been up in Cleveland would be doing their rehabilitation or taking some time in Akron or Columbus and how people would flock to them. He always felt ignored, but that was Marco. He was quick to superimpose intentions on others. Though sometimes he was right. The way people looked at him in the restaurant after the fly ball incident had never fully left the forefront of her mind. "And you want me to pitch a game?"

"That's correct," he said with a nod.

"Now, just to be up front here, would I be pitching as a member of the team or would this be a one time thing?"

"That depends on how well you do."

"You watched me pitch today. You've seen how good I am."

The scout shook his head. "I've seen you pitch against an entirely amateur team, let's see how you do against professionals and then we'll talk about your future."

A nagging voice in the back of Gioia's mind told her that meant she didn't have a future beyond this one single solitary game, but she forced that voice down. She listened only to the more optimistic voices that were loudly proclaiming this to be her chance, quite possibly her only chance, and if she didn't take it, she would never forgive herself. "Well, I think I can work with you."

His face broke into a smile. "That is exactly what I was hoping to hear."

Gioia nodded, still feeling very wary for the whole situation. "Now. What day? What time? What else do I need to do?"

With a a wave of his hand, he attempted to dismiss her concerns. "You let me sort all that out, Miss Rinaldi."

"I'm not very good with..." She began to protest.

He interrupted. "I know. I understand that. I just need to run this by the other promoters, get everything sorted out and make a few decisions. I'll call you and let you know the details when they get a little better solidified."

"You don't even have a date set?"

"I had to make sure you'd do it first."

She still wasn't sure she believed what was happening, but Gioia nodded. "How soon do you think you'll know?"

"It shouldn't be any longer than a week."

She mulled that over quickly. In a week, she would no longer be living in the dorm. "Do you have a pen?" He passed over a pen and flipped his steno pad to a blank page without a word. "This is my parent's number. Call it when you find out how things are going to be." It would be better this way. She wouldn't be alone when or if she got the call and she wouldn't get her hopes up if the call were to never come.

He took the steno pad back and flipped it shut dramatically. "You should hear from me in about a week." He strolled away appearing contented, but Gioia was still confused. She thought back to when Alta and Cy had brought that other ghost by the park. She wasn't sure, but maybe that had something to do with it. Maybe that meant that this really was happening after all. Still, she was far too afraid to allow herself to truly believe.

29

The stadium, though smaller than a Major League park, was everything Gioia imagined it would be. Both her parents stood warily by her side as they walked in. They all had their doubts as well as their hopes for what the day ahead might bring.

"Now, Gioia," her father began to say for the hundredth time since they got up that morning.

"I know, Padre. I know," Gioia answered immediately. She had thought out so many possible scenarios for the day. Most of them ended poorly. She knew well enough that these same scenarios were wearing on her father's mind. "I have to go meet them in the office. You two go find Marco and your seats."

He nodded and started off. Her mother stopped though. "Do they have a uniform for you? In your size? It doesn't have a skirt does it?"

"Madre," Gioia said sweetly, trying to calm her mother. "I have a uniform just like everyone else."

"And they have somewhere for you to change?"

"Madre, it's going to be fine." She assured her yet again. Mrs. Rinaldi nodded calmly. She hoped it would be. Gioia herself wasn't exactly sure, but she pretended that she was for her parent's sake. "Just go get your seats."

The Rinaldi parents did just that as Gioia started away, a pit growing in her stomach. She forced herself to only look forward. If she were to watch her parents disappear into the crowd, she knew that she might not be able to go through with it. There were so many ways that this could go horribly wrong. Maybe she was better off not knowing.

Gioia and the rest of the Rinaldi family didn't know many of the people in the crowd and they had never before met Audrey Dawson, who was about to walk irrevocably into their lives. When Audrey had initially pitched the idea to Mr. Fleming to come out and cover the game, he had been a bit unsure. Audrey understood his reluctance. She had never covered much in the way of the minor league teams, but after some consideration, she decided she was going to write the article either way.

She went right to the administration and press area. It was all significantly smaller than it was at Comerica Park, which she knew she should have been expecting. Peter Sullivan was waiting there for her. He jumped up to his feet immediately when she entered, which only served to make Audrey feel even more nervous than she had been already about walking into a strange place. "Miss Dawson!" He exclaimed excitedly.

Audrey shook his hand awkwardly, still not used to this sort of attention. "You must be Mr. Sullivan?"

"That's me. Now, you're here to talk to Miss Rinaldi? Is that correct?"

"She's here, isn't she?"

"Of course. She just doesn't know you are. Now if you'll just give me a moment..."

He stepped toward the door just as Gioia entered, dressed in a Lake County Captains uniform. "Mr. Sullivan, I was told you wanted to see me before the game began?" She asked, sounding just as nervous and confused as Audrey felt. Immediately, Audrey knew, somehow, that they would get along, if only for the fact that they both seemed to feel terribly isolated in this world they wanted to be part of.

Mr. Sullivan nodded toward Audrey. "I have a blogger here who would like to speak with you."

"A blogger?" Gioia asked skeptically.

Audrey moved past Mr. Sullivan and held out her hand. "My name's Audrey Dawson. I write for a baseball blog in Detroit called *This Urban Jungle*."

She was about to continue, but Gioia interrupted, a smirk on her face. "Detroit?"

Audrey nodded and glanced back at Mr. Sullivan, who backed away, letting her do the interview. "I typically cover big league news, but I do like to do features about baseball in general and I was thinking that a female player joining a mainstream team would be quite the feature."

Gioia smiled a bit, not able to deny that this made her feel validated. "Detroit though?" she asked teasingly when she was sure Mr. Sullivan was far enough away to not hear. "You know I thought I saw certain Rocky Colavito in the hall and he told me 'Don't do it. Don't go to them.'"

Audrey couldn't help laughing at that. "I somehow doubt that would be his advice."

Gioia shook her head, musing over the possibility for a moment. "Well, he's not going to be letting me know any time soon."

"Not being one of your ghosts?" Audrey asked, slightly conspiratorial. The two shared a knowing nod.

"So...what do you want to talk about?" Gioia asked carefully. She still wasn't feeling too terribly confident, but Audrey seemed nice enough to talk to.

"How do you feel about tonight?"

With another look around to make sure Mr. Sullivan was unseen, Gioia began. "Well it's been a long time coming, but I'm still not one hundred percent sure about the whole thing."

"And why's that?"

"You ever have something happen to you that you simply couldn't believe was true?"

Audrey had to admit that was the case, thinking back on her recent success in online media. "Every day of my life."

"I guess that pretty much sums it up, then."

She looked at her notebook. She was sure that statement itself was enough to spin an entire article out of. She didn't need anything more, but she wanted more. This article was important and it needed to shine. "Would I be able to talk to you after the game as well?"

"Getting sure you have the exclusive scoop now?" Gioia teased.

"Something like that."

Gioia nodded. "They'll probably pull me after the first inning when I get laughed off the field. I'll come chat with you about it then."

Audrey shook her head. "Don't talk like that. A lot of people are counting on you."

"On me? They don't even know me."

"They don't have to."

Both girls were quiet, considering this a moment. Gioia had tried to force away any feelings about what this meant to her or, even more importantly, anyone other than her. Mr. Sullivan had presented pitching this game to her as a novelty, something to be joked about, something to be experienced and seen like a sideshow. She knew from the way he talked that he saw her as something akin to the weight lifters or half horse-half fish exhibits in old fashioned circuses. She was a show. That was all she was meant to be. He wasn't planning on letting her stay on the the team no matter how many times he said, "We'll see how you do and go from there." She knew what was going to happen in the end. Knowing that made feeling like she was doing something groundbreaking impossible.

She hadn't told her parents or brother about this feeling, but the fact that this reporter seemed to think of her as someone who could be an inspiration to others made her cringe. She knew she wasn't going to be. She was going to be a flash in the pan, nothing more than a foot note.

"Have you ever heard of Jackie Mitchell?" Gioia began.

"I vaguely recall her, yes," Audrey replied sarcastically, already knowing where this was probably going and trying to build a mental defense against it.

"A lot of baseball historians say that she was a gimmick. That the strikeouts were planned by the Chattanooga Lookouts."

Audrey nodded. "I've heard that before, but why did Babe Ruth get so angry if he knew it was going to happen?"

Gioia admitted she had always wondered, but it was a theory she had been thinking about a lot since Mr. Sullivan had asked her to pitch. "A lot of people still say it."

"A lot of people are going to say a lot of things. You can't always listen to them." Audrey found herself saying before she had really thought about her words. They were her father's words to her on numerous occasions. It felt strange to be echoing him, though she knew well enough that he would have said the same.

"I try."

"You should see some of the comments I get on my blog. They're sexist and awful, but I have to keep writing. It's the one thing I love. I can't let them take that away from me."

Gioia actually broke into a smile and extended her hand again to shake Audrey's, this time a little more confidently. This time she saw Audrey not as a reporter, but an ally, in exactly the way Audrey saw her. "I imagine," was all she really could say, though she was thinking a great deal more. She could definitely imagine the sort of comments Audrey would get, but if she could push that aside...

Mr. Sullivan quickly moved back toward the two girls. "I hate to interrupt the gab session, ladies..." Gioia and Audrey both bristled a bit at that. "But Miss Rinaldi here has to get out there on the field and show them how it's done."

Gioia nodded, taking a deep breath. "Here goes nothing."

Audrey closed her notebook. "Finish after the game?'

"You're on," Gioia replied with a definitive nod.

"Knock 'em dead?"

"I'll try." She took another deep breath and slipped out the door to join the rest of the team. It was time for now or never.

Knock them dead, she did. She walked out in the fourth inning as a reliever. She understood this, despite the fact that Mr. Sullivan said that she would start. It was asking a little much for him to put aside the other starters for her. She also didn't want to engender any negative feelings among her teammates. So it was in the fourth that she was announced and walked out to far more applause than she had been expecting.

The park was strange. She hadn't played in it before and the set up was very different than what she was used to; she tried not to let it faze her. She didn't want to look around among the crowd as an old fear was tugging at her from her high school days, but she couldn't help it. She had to look out and see. Her parents and Marco had very good seats behind home plate. It may not have been a Major League game, but Mr. Rinaldi seemed to be particularly pleased with the situation. He finally got to sit behind home plate somewhere.

Alta and Cy and an entire group of countless others were there. She could name some, but there were so many she couldn't even see them all. They had crowded into all of the aisles and stood along the edges of the field. There were so many. Most of the crowd didn't notice, but it was very clear that some of the people in the stands were amazed by their company.

Also in the stands was what appeared to be a girls' little league team. They had their eyes riveted to her; they didn't even seem able to blink. Despite all of the spirits surrounding her, they were the most moving to see.

After seeing and taking in all of this, she closed her eyes and shut it out, just as Cy had coached. She turned the cheers and jeers into a sort of silence, focused on the catcher and let these people suddenly become the only ones in the world. She turned it all off and pitched a strike.

She pitched for another two innings before they brought in another reliever. When she went into the dugout, though something was nagging at her about wanting to pitch longer, she still felt that she had accomplished a great deal. The others on the team applauded. "Great job," said the starting pitcher. A few others echoed agreement.

"Thanks," she forced as a reply, feeling a blush beginning to grow on her cheeks. It was less out of embarrassment and more from the rush of emotions and pride she was feeling.

Audrey was waiting there, notebook in hand. "Good game," she said when Gioia sat down next to her.

Gioia simply shook her head. "It's not over yet."

"Of course..." Audrey nodded, looking out at the field. "It's going to be a close one, looks like."

"Not my fault."

Audrey smirked. "Proud of your performance, I take it?"

Gioia nodded, looking out at the field as well, watching what her hopefully soon to be teammates made of the rest of the game. "Decent."

"Think it'll be good enough?" Though she didn't specify, Gioia knew exactly what she meant by that.

"I'll have to wait and see. We can only hope."

EPILOGUE

THIS URBAN JUNGLE
JUNE 15: A NEW BASEBALL QUEEN TO REIGN

Recently, I had the pleasure of witnessing something that I had never even considered I might do. Oftentimes, baseball firsts and true greatness seem relegated to the past. They're stuck back in another time with the ghosts that walk among us. They are the dominion of Ty Cobb, Babe Ruth, and Joe DiMaggio and not something that we in this modern era of baseball can truly call our own. In some ways we are wrong. We are deeply wrong.

We live in a world that can still break and set new records, that can create new legends, and can do exactly as I saw last Saturday at a West Michigan Whitecaps game against the Lake County Captains. I saw Gioia Rinaldi become the first female pitcher in over a decade take the mound for the Captains.

Now, I know that as they are a Detroit Tigers minor league affiliate, my true loyalty must lie with the Whitecaps and of course I can tell you that our West Michigan boys performed valiantly. I also must tell you that the three innings in which Gioia Rinaldi were pitching were some of the best moments, I personally have experienced in baseball.

Some of you may not comprehend this and that's all right. I can't blame you at all. It's hard to feel something that you don't understand. You might even take this statement as siding with someone based solely on their gender, which I will tell you straight away is wrong and shouldn't be done. What also shouldn't be done is siding against someone solely because of their gender. I have seen a lot of that in the world of sport.

I have seen comments on my articles that say such insightful things as "You're a female what would you know?" and "WOMEN DON'T KNOW BASEBALL!!" There have even been quite vulgar comments that throw any bit of attractiveness or perceived lack there of back into my face as though it somehow invalidates my opinions. It can be very grating to have such things spewed in your direction, just for attempting to discuss the thing you love with others who presumably love the same thing.

Gioia Rinaldi told me she had faced similar and I can only imagine. For a woman in sport to be taken seriously, it is indeed a struggle. She said that from a young age she knew that not only that she had to be better than all of the other girls, but she had to be better than all of the boys as well. She had to be ten times better than the boys, otherwise she would be written off far too easily. She said that she always knew that if she individually failed it was not just a failure for herself, but a failure for all women as her inability to perform would be taken as all omen's inability to perform. This drove her youthful ambitions to work harder than ever and become the best pitcher she could be.

Her road was not a conventional one. While her brother was recruited to the minor leagues in high school, she had nary a scout until she went to college and formed her own inter-mural team that practiced regularly in League Park, an old stadium that had once been the home of the various Cleveland baseball clubs in ages past. The park itself is a legend. The first pitch thrown there was delivered by Cy Young and it was the place where female pitcher Alta Weiss debuted. Perhaps it was only fitting that Gioia Rinaldi needed to come to this place first before moving on with her pitching career.

And perhaps that's why we understand each other. As a writer, I wasn't able to take the typical sportswriter's road through the paper that I had worked on as many of those who stood in my shoes before me had done. I had to create this blog, my own space in which to do so. I had to make this creation work for me on my own.

Despite the struggles, we both faced in getting here, there is something in the air that seems to be finally moving this forward as it should. As I witnessed Gioia Rinaldi strike out six straight batters and only allow two hits, I knew we were on to something. She handled the ball masterfully with a fastball that could break fingers and a baffling curve. Maybe they weren't expecting her abilities at first, but she had truly given a strong answer of yes to the question of "Can a women hold her own against men in a game of professional baseball?" Though I'm sure the yes had been given before and will be given again, Gioia Rinaldi made it very clear Saturday night that her yes was going to be heard.

ABOUT THE AUTHOR

Amy Stilgenbauer is an information scientist, freelance writer, and baseball aficionado, who spends her life split between Ohio and Michigan; the two places where she fell deeply in love with America's National Pastime. She received her degree in writing from Mount Union College in 2007. This is her first novel.

Made in the USA
Lexington, KY
01 December 2012